MR. CONTROL

A SINGLE DAD ROMANCE

MAYA HUGHES

Copyright © 2017 by Maya Hughes

All rights reserved.

No part of this book may be reproduced in any form or by any electronic or mechanical means, including information storage and retrieval systems, without written permission from the author, except for the use of brief quotations in a book review.

Cover Designer: LJ Anderson, Mayhem Cover Creations

PREFACE

"When love awakens in your life, in the night of your heart, it is like the dawn breaking within you....where before you used to be jagged, now you are elegant and in rhythm with yourself. When love awakens in your life, it is like a rebirth, a new beginning."

— <u>John O'Donohue</u>, <u>Anam Cara: A Book of Celtic Wisdom</u>

1

RHYS

"We would like a round of applause for one of our most generous benefactors to the Ashton Foundation, Mr. Rhys Thayer," said the rotund man with the bright red cheeks. I stood, buttoning my suit jacket and waving to the crowd as applause filled the room. You'd have thought the announcer just ran a mile in six minutes flat, the way sweat poured down his face and soaked through his shirt right at the center of his chest. But no, he'd just walked up a few steps to the top of the stage. The man, what was his name? Gary? Grant? Graham? It didn't matter anyway.

The G man went for a handshake, pumping so hard, like he wanted to detach my fucking hand from my arm. I gripped him by the shoulder, keeping that stupid smile plastered on my face, and squeezed. Grant/Gary/Graham released my hand from his sweaty grip and I wiped it on my suit pants that probably cost more than this guy's toupee. At least I hadn't paid for them.

"Would you like to give a speech?" the G man said, spittle flying in my face.

"No, that's quite all right. I wouldn't want to keep everyone from enjoying their wonderful lunch. Plus, I'm sure everyone would much rather listen to the beautiful song that's been prepared rather than have me squawk up here," I said. In three, two, one, peals of laughter broke out across the crowd. It wasn't even a funny joke. But when you had money like me, it didn't matter. I could whip out my dick out and piss on someone sitting in the front row and they'd applaud.

Derek appeared by the side of the stage to escort me out. Saved by the fucking bell. The music swelled and some opera singer took the stage and belted out her song. I excused myself and made my way down the stairs at the back of the stage.

"What took you so long?"

"I had to make sure Esme was settled in okay with Hunter before I left," Derek said, keeping his eyes forward as he led me out of the hotel. He needed to lighten up. I hadn't received a death threat in months.

"How was she?" I asked, matching my stride with Derek's, which was quite a feat considering that Derek dwarfed me by at least four inches even though I'm six two.

"She was fine. He was going to take her to the toy store."

"Okay, good. That's a great way for him to ingratiate himself with her."

"Did she say anything when you left?"

Derek shot me a hard glance. "You know what I mean," he said, shrugging. Esme hadn't spoken to anyone but me since the day she'd been found next to her mother's body. Derek was the only other person alive who knew that fact.

"No. She didn't." And that was the end of the conversation. Derek held open the door to the black SUV and I climbed in. Next stop, the bank. You'd think the life of a billionaire philanthropist leant itself to lots of free time, but it felt like all I did was get shuttled from meeting to meeting, event to event, gala to gala. I hadn't had a day off in the past six months. It drained every ounce of energy I had. Especially when I hated every minute of it.

2

MEL

The din of chatter and silverware clinking filled the air. The pungent smell of carbs and coffee clung to every surface in the diner, including my uniform. I tucked my pen behind my ear as I stood in front of my eighth table this shift. At least tips would be good with so many tables packed in my section. The middle-aged couple at my table continued to flip through their menu. I'd visited this table three times now waiting for them to order. I could cut to the chase and let them know that whatever they chose would suck. The only thing that kept this restaurant open was the prime NYC location luring in a continual flow of unsuspecting tourists with their wallets wide open.

Martin reminded us time and time again that customers came to the diner for the atmosphere, not the food. I glanced around at the cracked tiles and dingy paint, tapping my foot. He was a greedy little weasel who capitalized on the fact that he'd allowed a movie to film in the diner ages ago. He'd been trading on that little gem for decades.

"We'll have the—" *Yes, finally!* My enthusiasm of finally

getting an order out of them was cut short by the clattering of a chair behind me. I spun and caught a streak of blue as the customers from my fifth table of the evening dashed out the front door. *Fuck.* I dropped my note pad on the table and raced after them, my sneakers squealing on the broken tiles as I pushed through the door.

Martin was crystal clear about the waitress' responsibility when it came to dine and dashers. As in, it was our complete and total responsibility to stop them and if they got away, well, that came out of our paychecks. Totally illegal, but there wasn't much choice other than quitting.

The frigid wind and raindrops stung my face as I pushed through the crowds of people with umbrellas wandering aimlessly down the sidewalk. *Out of the way.* The temptation to start body checking old ladies grew strong as the bright blue jacket of the guy I chased got farther and farther out of sight.

One second I spotted a gap in the crowd and bolted for it, and the next, the world tilted as I slammed my knees into the hard, cold, wet sidewalk.

"Ahh!" I yelped as the crowds surged past me like a rock plunked down in the middle of a river. The rain kicked up a notch and pelted me. The concrete dug into my palms, scraping them as I pushed myself up. I glanced down as a thin trail of blood rolled down my shin. My leg throbbing, I cursed the rain and the asshole who skipped out on the check. I limped off to the side of the sidewalk and found a dry spot under an awning. Shielded from the elements, even a little, I lifted my knee to check out the damage.

"Hey, baby, looking good," someone from the surging crowd called out. I dropped my leg, suddenly aware of how short my uniform skirt was and the fact that I hadn't found any clean underwear, so I had gone without that day. I flipped the bird to no one in particular as people flowed by. I hope whoever had called out to me had enjoyed the show.

My pantyhose was ripped and there were a few runs along the length of my leg. Martin required all his waitresses to wear pantyhose, like we were living in the '70s. I'd have to stop off and buy a new pair from the corner shop. I leaned my head against the brick wall behind me—and got out some money to pay the check of the dashers. *Dammit.* Today was not shaping up to be my day. Just like every other day this year.

I limped down the sidewalk, wrapping my arms around myself as icy rain hit me and stabbed right through my cheap pink uniform. On my way back to the diner, I came to a bank and popped inside their toasty vestibule to use the ATM. I slipped my card in, rubbing my hands together and breathing into them. My warm breath temporarily thawed my fingers enough to punch in my pin. A twenty should cover the food and some new hose. A blinking blue message flashed on the screen, "Insufficient Funds." I checked my balance. Less than twelve dollars. That didn't make any sense. My breath caught in my chest.

I punched in the numbers again. There had to be a mistake. Again, the same flashing screen popped up. I still didn't understand it. I'd had over three hundred dollars in there last week. I gritted my teeth as tears welled in my eyes. I hated crying. And I hated even more that when I got pissed, I cried. It was an involuntary reflex that had given me so much trouble over the years. I told Colleen not to touch this account without letting me know first. She rambled on about not having the card anyway. She hadn't touched it in over a year, and I hadn't had enough money to open a new account anywhere else. The sting of regret ran through me. I rested my head against the cold metal of the ATM and retrieved my card.

The door behind me opened. A cold blast shot straight down my spine as goosebumps peppered my skin, making my wet uniform even more uncomfortable. *What the hell was I going to do now?* A white, delicately embroidered handkerchief appeared under my nose and I jerked my head away. Standing beside me with her arm outstretched was a little girl.

"For your boo-boo," she said, pointing to my leg. The blood had congealed some on my knee, but the long drips of blood had stained through the pantyhose.

She couldn't have been more than six or seven. She looked up at me with her big, bright blue eyes and motioned with the handkerchief. Raindrops sat on her hat and coat. The water didn't seep in and soak through her clothes, as it did mine. Instead, it rolled right off.

"Thanks, kid, but I'll be okay," I said, crumpling the ATM receipt and dropping it into the trash can as I headed toward the door.

"For your boo-boo," she repeated and followed me, insisting I take it. I felt bad. I didn't want to get blood on this super nice piece of fabric.

"Thanks," I said, taking the handkerchief from her. *What the hell was she doing with a handkerchief anyway?* Weren't these only for people fifty and above? I ran my fingers over the thick, luxurious fabric. This thing probably cost more than I made in a week. I took a closer look at the little girl. If ever there were a kid to walk around with a lush handkerchief, it was her.

"Where are your parents, kiddo?" She shrugged.

She had on an adorable navy pea coat, dark tights, soaked ballet flats and an honest-to-God beret on top of her sandy brown hair, with a mini purse slung across her body. *Who was this kid?* I glanced around, trying to spot her parents.

"You shouldn't do that. You shouldn't run away from people who care about you," I snapped, nausea rolling through me as I thought about how much trouble she could have gotten into. She shrank back and I cringed. *Chill out.* I took a deep breath, relaxed, and bent down to her.

"Sorry, kiddo. I just don't want you to get hurt." I scanned the people walking around on the other side of the glass vestibule. I looked for someone who looked like they were searching frantically, but everyone as far as I could see just milled around, umbrellas up, doing their own thing. I checked my phone. I needed to get back to the diner before Martin had my head, but I didn't want to leave her here. Indecision warred in me as I peered down at her. I'd have to take her with me and hope we ran into her mom or dad on the way back to the diner. I didn't want her getting picked up by the cops. Who knows what kind of shitstorm could rain down on her.

"Which way did you come from?" I asked, crouching down in front of her. I winced at the throbbing pain in my knee. The aching registered as I warmed up inside the bank. She turned and pointed back down the street toward the diner. Okay, that helped some. I'd have to take her with me and hope we ran into her mom or dad on the way there.

"Were your parents in the bank?" I asked, glancing back through the glass. She shook her head furiously.

"My name is Melanie, but my friends call me Mel. What's your name?" I held out my hand for her to shake it. She slid her warm little hand into mine.

"Esme. My name is Esme." Her squeaky little voice made me smile. She was a cute kid.

"Okay, Esme. Let's go. We'll go to the diner where I work and keep you warm while we figure out where your parents are. Maybe we'll pass them on the way."

"My daddy," she squeaked out.

"Your daddy?" I said, holding onto her hand. She nodded. "Great, we'll find your daddy and get you back home safe and sound. How does that sound?" I paused in front of the door and prepared myself for another cold blast. She gripped my hand tighter, and I squeezed right back.

"Don't worry, it's only a couple of blocks and we'll be there before you know it. Do you like hot chocolate?" I asked. Her eyes lit up, sparkling under the glare of the vestibule light. She could have my food from this shift. I was sure she was scared out of her mind. "Let's go, kiddo," I said, whipping the door open. The frigid air hit us, but the rain had let up, so it was only drizzling. She gripped my hand tightly as we hustled back to the diner. I'd have to go without the pantyhose. If Martin wanted to throw a fit, he could go buy me another pair.

I kept my eye out for anyone frantic as we walked back the couple of blocks to the diner. We pushed through the door and it was business as usual inside. Jeanine covered my tables, and Martin must have been hanging in his office. If he knew what happened, he would have been standing at the register, holding up the check my customer skipped out on, and demanding I pay it right then. I'd be able to scrape by with enough tips to cover it by the end of my shift. Jeanine's eyebrow quirked up seeing Esme's hand in mine. I shrugged my shoulders and got Esme situated on one of the stools at the counter.

"Why don't you hop up here?" I said, lifting her up. She

clambered up onto the seat and spun around, looking very out of place in the rundown diner. Someone was probably having a fit over her going missing. I knew all about that. My stomach dropped as I thought about how horrible a feeling that was. "How about some hot chocolate?" I asked her. She nodded, and I called out to Jim for a mug of the warm, chocolatey treat. It was probably the only thing in the whole place that wasn't horrible. He gave me a sweaty nod and went to work.

"I'll be right back. Okay?" I said. Her hand shot out and gripped mine tightly, squeezing my fingers together. She had quite a grip. "Hey, it's okay. I'm just going to go right over there to my friend. See her?" I said, pointing at Jeanine, who shot back and forth from table to table. "I'm going to go help her out. She's doing me a favor by waiting on those tables for me, and I don't want to upset her."

"Okay," she squeaked out, so low it was barely a whisper.

"Thanks, Esme." I rushed over to Jeanine. She shot me a glare and I cringed.

"Did a little sightseeing? And picked up a stray?" she said, bustling past me into the kitchen. *Looks like my share of the tips would be a lot smaller tonight.* But I owed her. Jim slid a cup of hot chocolate to Esme across the counter. She lifted it up and took a small sip. A big smile spread across her face as she tried to lick off the whipped cream she'd gotten all over her chin. Clearly a bit happier, she kicked her feet and spun slowly on the stool.

I rushed back and forth from table to table, bringing out the orders that were placed while I was out, and cleaning up as customers left. Every so often I'd shoot a glance to Esme and another out the window, looking for anyone freaking out about a missing child. Droves of people passed by, and a few people came in for a meal. Other than that, it was like any other day.

Esme seemed perfectly content to hang out on the stool, spinning around some and drawing a picture or two on the placemats with some crayons I'd scrounged up from the back. No one spoke to her and she didn't speak to anyone else. I couldn't help but wonder where she came from, or how long I should wait to call the cops. Plus, I didn't want to get anyone in trouble. A sharp pang stomach, and I wrapped my arms around myself.

Sometimes, kids make mistakes. They get angry and run away, never thinking about the consequences of what they've done. Not considering how it could change the course of their entire life in a moment. I knew how the mistakes of children could be held against them – even ruin their life. I didn't want anything like that to happen to Esme.

I popped of the kitchen with an armload of plates, all ready for my biggest table of the night, when I saw a hulking man in a dark suit standing in front of Esme, trying to talk to her. He had a short buzz cut and wore sunglasses, despite the rainy weather. Esme scrunched herself up against the counter, not looking happy to see him. *Who the hell was this guy?* Everything happened so quickly. One second he tried to grab her, and in the next I dumped my plates down on the nearest table and threw myself between them.

I planted myself in front of her and pushed him back with both hands as hard as I could.

"Hey, don't you fucking touch her," I hissed, getting right in his face. He didn't even flinch as his shaded gaze snapped to me. "Do you hear me? Back off," I said, pushing him back again. He didn't shift an inch as my hands met his solid chest. My pulse began to pound. *Who was this guy? Why was he talking to Esme? Was she in danger?* More and more questions flew through my head as I glared up at the unflinching man with the earpiece. Esme slid her hand into mine. I turned to give her a reassuring smile when the front door was flung open with an alarming bang that made me jump and put my arm protectively around Esme. *What the hell was going on?* I tried to peer around the asshole towering over me.

"There you are," came a voice smoother than silk, even though I could hear a note of the frantic anxiety that only losing a kid will create in a parent. A brute of a man rushed in, flanked by another huge guy in a black suit. This one had dark brown hair that was longer on top. I named him Hulk #2. Esme leaned to the side to get a better view, and a tall man with chestnut hair rushed forward. His expensive cologne wafted by, scenting the air with something other than pancakes, burgers, and coffee. He smelled better than any man I'd ever encountered. Hulk #1 escorted Hulk #2 out of the diner, and by that I mean he practically threw him out the front door.

Before I even knew what was happening, Mr. Cologne had his arms wrapped around Esme, and she hugged him back.

"Are you okay?" the man asked, crouching down and squeezing her in a hug. "Don't do that to me, sweetie."

As he turned with her in his arms, everything suddenly made more sense. I was face to face with Rhys Thayer, one of the richest and most powerful men in the world. Also one of the most generous, from what I've read, but he wasn't feeling generous right then.

Kissing the top of Esme's head, he kept his gaze on me and I was definitely aware of the scrutiny. My fingers tingled and I wanted to take a step back, but I was frozen. He pinned me with his stare, eyes burning into mine. What happened to the good-natured philanthropist I'd seen so many news features about? His eyes were laser-focused on me and I finally took a step back. For a second, the intimidating mask slipped when he glanced at Esme wrapped up in his arms. Searing my skin, he gave me the once over, glaring at me like he could destroy me at any moment. *Maybe he could.*

3

RHYS

Smiles and handshakes. It seemed that's all my life was at this point. My hard work at continuing my parent's legacy had paid off, to the detriment of my personal life, except for Esme. She changed my life in a way I hadn't thought possible. When the doctors first laid her in my arms, it made my purpose in life sharper, clearer, as far as what I needed to do to keep her safe. I'd been given a fortune bigger than most people could imagine, and at the age of eighteen I was in control of sums of money that could transform lives. Which meant I controlled lives, lives of adults, and that kind of power in the hands of any kid was dangerous. It split my personality in some ways. In front of the crowds and cameras, I was one way but, behind closed doors, it was another story. A side of me I couldn't let out often, not in the brightness of day. It was a side of me that had scared more than one woman away, which cemented my decision to keep those encounters as close to professional as possible, setting boundaries for them and for me. If I allowed myself to truly unleash, I don't know if there was a woman out there who could handle me.

"Sir, we have a situation," Derek said, pulling me aside from the handshake carousel I was continuously on. Things moved in slow motion as I raced out of the boardroom, knocking a few suits out of the way.

Fear does not begin to describe the feeling that coursed through me as my security team and I turned the city upside down looking for Esme. She knew better than to run off. I'd been at the bank, setting up a trust for a foundation I'd donated to, and I brought her along. We were going to a show after and it would make things easier. Plus, I hated leaving her on her own for so long. The day Esme was born was one of the happiest of my life. I still remember that glowing ball of joy that welled up inside me as I held her in my arms for the first time.

The happiness of that experience only made the gut punch of what I'd learned two years later that much harder to bear. But today would rank right up there as one of the worst days of my life. Esme wasn't known for wandering off or being able to shake her security. But how many six-year-olds had their own security detail? I couldn't take chances with her. I wouldn't. Her disappearing act had me calling in every person I knew, monitoring every radio frequency, and I was even working on getting someone on tracking cell signals when security spotted her through the window of a diner. I've never run so fast in my life. My feet pounded against the pavement, jarring shocks running through my body as I slid into the diner.

I didn't even stop to evaluate the scene. Derek stood in front of a woman, who stood in front of Esme and she was my concern. I scooped my daughter up in my arms and breathed her in. She smelled like chocolate and coffee. She looked up at me with big wide eyes and a huge smile. I smiled even though I internally jumped back and forth between wanting to yell at her never to do that again, and deciding I was never letting her out of my sight again, now that she was safe.

"Don't ever do that to me again," I said, forcefully. She nodded and whispered a 'sorry daddy' with her arms wrapped around my neck. My heart rate finally returning to normal, I turned to the woman who had been between Derek and Esme. A waitress. A waitress who worked here in the diner from the looks of the other people standing around. *Had Esme wandered into the diner?* The waitress had a big scrape on her knee and her stockings were ripped. Her rich mahogany eyes went through a few different stages of emotion, anger, surprise, then recognition. Ah yes, she knew who I was. And what I wanted to know now was what the hell she'd done with my daughter. And now a new emotion sprung up in her eyes, fear. Good, I wanted to ensure her cooperation in whatever came next.

"Rhys Thayer," I said, extending my hand to hers. She wiped her palm on her dingy pink skirt.

"Mel. Melanie Bright," she said, shaking my hand. Her small hand felt like spun glass in my hand, although her demeanor screamed tough chick. She fidgeted with the hem of her skirt.

"How did you end up with my daughter, Ms. Bright?" *Had she coerced her from wherever she found her? Had Esme come into the diner?* My mind cycled through all the horrible scenarios I'd created in my head in the two hours Esme had been missing. Especially since Esme wouldn't have cried out for help.

"I was getting money out of the ATM, and I think Esme saw I was hurt and wanted to help." She kept talking, but nothing registered in my mind after she said Esme's name.

Had the other security guard said it to her before I got there?

"So she wandered away to help you? Someone she's never met?"

"I don't lie," she said, through gritted teeth. "I didn't know where she came from. She just pushed through the door and she was there."

"And you just walked away with her?" I growled.

"No," she said, putting her hands on her hips. "I didn't just walk away with her. I asked her where her parents were. And she said it was just her dad," she continued, but my brain froze at that statement. Esme said it was just her dad. Esme didn't talk to anyone but me. The waitress kept talking. I must have misheard her. "—stood around waiting for someone who looked like they lost her and then asked her which direction she came from. She pointed this way, so I figured we might run into her dad on the way back. Esme and I came back to the diner. I got her a cup of her favorite drink, hot chocolate, and she's just been hanging out with me. Right, Esme?"

"How did you know hot chocolate was her favorite?" I know there's a lot of information out there about me and Esme, but I was pretty sure that wasn't something that had ever come up. *How did she know that? Who was she? Had she found a way to lure Esme away?* I raced through several ways to protect my daughter from whatever this threat might be and stepped in front of Esme.

Melanie stopped short with whatever she was saying and tilted her head to the side. She eyed me quizzically. "She told me," she said, looking at me like I was the biggest moron she'd ever spoken to. *Esme spoke to her?* That sentence seemed so strange in my own head that I had to roll over it a few times. It came out stilted as I said it out loud.

"Esme spoke to you?"

"Yes, she gave me this handkerchief for the cut on my knee," she said, producing one of mine from her pocket and gesturing to her leg. "And said it was for my boo-boo and then she told me her name." I glanced from Esme, whose tiny fingers gripped onto three of mine, and back to Melanie. I had to revise my initial assessment of her. Her mussed mop of light brown hair flew in different directions as she hustled from table to table.

Her eyes were what struck me first, bright and friendly, although they were quite wary right now. She came up to my shoulder, which meant she was taller than average for a woman, since I was over six feet. Athletic, with some curves. Cute even, spunky probably. Someone who would turn heads when she walked into a room, but not even notice. But the thing that intrigued me most was that she'd connected with my daughter, who had only ever spoken to me in the past three years.

"She hasn't spoken to anyone other than me in over three years."

Another head tilt. She glanced from me to Esme.

"She hasn't?" she said, squinting like she was trying to piece together the same puzzle I was. *Why had Esme decided to speak to her?*

"No, she hasn't," I said, trying to figure her out.

"Wow, in that case," she said, crouching down, "I am really glad you decided to speak to me when you got lost, Esme. That was very brave of you." She smiled and Esme lit up. The smile she gave Melanie reached all the way there. I hadn't seen one of those in a long time.

"Thank you for the hot chocolate, Mel," Esme whispered, low enough that only the three of us could make it out. She tentatively stepped out from behind me and flung herself at Melanie and wrapped her arms around her waist. Derek's phone clattered to the ground beside me. I don't think he'd ever heard her speak before. Derek glanced over at me and I nodded. I wanted to know everything there was to know about Melanie Bright and I wanted that information yesterday. I needed to figure out why she seemed to be the key to unlocking Esme from the world she'd closed herself inside.

"Thank you for looking after my daughter. Someone will be in touch with you shortly," I said, turning to head out with Esme's hand firmly in mine. We'd have to have a talk about running off with strangers.

"In touch about what?" she asked, her hand shooting out to grab my arm. I glanced down at her hand where she grasped me. Her warmth seeped through my suit jacket even on this cold day. I looked up, meeting her eyes and she quickly pulled her hand back. I bit back my reflex to put it back. I didn't know who the hell this woman was, but I would find out.

"There will be a nondisclosure agreement someone will send by that you'll need to sign." This could be a big problem for me. For Esme. Everything about our lives needed to be picture perfect and having her run away and get lost would not play well to anyone. A host of non-disclosure agreements and other documents would be on their way to Mel to ensure our lives weren't disrupted by someone who might want to do us harm.

"Wait—" she said, trying to follow after us, but we were already gone. We walked out of the diner and stepped into a waiting town car. At home, after a long talk with Esme about never doing anything like that ever again, I put her to bed and sat down in my study. Glass of scotch in my hand, I nursed it and thought back to the waitress from the no-name diner. Melanie. I rolled her name over in my mind.

Derek dropped off a folder with her whole life story in it a little while ago. Grew up in the Midwest, a few run-ins with the police over things like shoplifting when she was younger. A screwed-up childhood that included some time in the foster-care system. Her home life was about as far away from mine as you could get, but growing up like I had, maybe we had more in common than I thought. The rest of the file contained a few red flags, but nothing major. Moved to NYC a few years ago, bounced around from job to job. No college, no career, no real prospects. *So why had Esme decided to open up to her?*

My life as the poor little rich boy meant my friends were few and family nonexistent. My parents hadn't known they would die in their forties, but their wishes for the money they left me were clear. So clear, I wondered if they'd ever seen me as more than an extension of their legacy. I didn't want that for Esme. She'd know I loved her, cared about her as my daughter, not as another vehicle for my life's mission. Which meant she'd always be my little girl, but she'd have to leave like everyone else in my life left. The pain that drove through me washed away, seeing her grow and flourish. Which was why I needed to figure out Melanie Bright. *Was she the key to fixing whatever broke inside my little girl? Would she be the key to helping her with troubles on the horizon?*

Esme didn't speak to anyone. Anyone but me, that is. For the past three years, since her mother died, she'd been virtually mute. She's so smart, did well in school, but will not speak to anyone else. I've taken her to every specialist I could think of, every psychologist, psychiatrist, everyone says it's okay for her to have experienced trauma related to her mother's death. That she'll come out of it when she's ready, but I know that's not true.

I know she's seen things no child should ever see. My hand and fingers were tingling, throbbing as the anger warred with shame. I did everything I could, short of committing my wife to get her better, to keep her safe, but money combined with access meant the temptations Beth faced were nearly insurmountable. My biggest regret was that she'd managed to expose Esme to any of it. She lulled me into a false sense of security, I thought it was all behind her. I'd let her take Esme that day. Mother-daughter bonding she'd said. I'd been too damn stupid to see her slips. I thought I had it all under control. I'd been wrong. I'd been so fucking wrong and now my little girl paid the price.

The prickling heat that built up whenever I thought of that day reached a boiling point. I felt better for a second, letting the fire race through me. The tight reins have come off for just a little bit. But then I slam on the brakes. I must maintain my image, not only to protect myself, but to protect my daughter. There are so many ways this can go wrong. I worry that it isn't a phase and she won't grow into the woman I envision, leading a happy and healthy life. I'm determined, though. And that day will come.

One day she'll grow up. And I'll be all alone again. All alone with the regrets of my life. All alone with money that wasn't mine to spend, only mine to give away, and I'll have no one to share my life with. But my daughter deserves to have a real shot at a life, not the fishbowl existence I was born into.

I'd tried to make things work with a couple of women after my wife. I thought maybe a mother figure would help Esme recover, but once they knew the strings attached to my money, my life didn't seem so glamorous anymore. And once I saw how many people walked away after they knew, I wasn't going to expose Esme to anyone else who wasn't going to stick around. So I stopped talking and started using, using them like they intended to use me.

Trust wasn't something that came easily to someone in my position. Someone with my background. Widower and single father. A man who required far too much from a woman to find it all with one. Everyone on the outside sees me as the prince of my own tale, but they don't know me. They don't know what my life has been like and they don't know the beast that rages inside.

And after six nannies, from the best recommendations, over the past three years, they were never the right fit. Never able to connect with my daughter, not like a waitress off the street had. I sent a text to my assistant. There would be some changes happening tomorrow. I checked on Esme again before slipping into the gym. The lap pool called to me. I stripped down and dove in. The warm water soothed me as I threw myself into the laps. Stroke after stroke, the water rushing over me as I kick flipped turn after turn.

Passing out at my desk in the wee hours or swimming laps until my legs were like leaden weights, threatening to pull me under; those were the only ways I could sleep most nights. The only way to pass out in my bed before my head hit the pillows. It also kept the clawing, bone-chilling nightmares at bay.

4
MEL

The key stuck in the lock to Jeanine's third-story, walk-up apartment, as it did every day. The peeling paint on the door was probably white at one point, but now it was a special shade of off-white that only came with decades of cigarette smoke and other colorful vapors seeping into every nook and cranny. I couldn't really complain since it wasn't even technically my place. I had to ram my shoulder into the door before it finally popped free and I burst into the living room. I guess you could call it a living room, it was more like a closet.

There was a mishmash of furniture from off the street, online sales and scrounged up from anyplace else that meant free or damn near close. The window looked out onto a weathered brick wall, leaving the apartment dark at any hour of the day. But again, I was just happy for a roof over my head. Beggars can't be choosers and all that.

Jeanine came out of the bathroom, rubbing her hair with a towel.

"Heard there was some excitement after I left for the day?"

"The little girl I brought in? Let me tell you," I threw my bag on the counter.

"You mean the stray?" she asked, in that snotty voice of hers that made me want to smack her. I glared at her and she shrank back.

"What?" she said, holding up her hands. If I hadn't known she was harmless and that she had made sure Esme's mug was always filled to the brim with hot chocolate, I'd have punched her. She was my best friend in the city, pretty much my only friend in the city. Which was pretty sad because I don't think she thought of me as more than her own version of a stray. Once I started working at the diner, she gave me a place to crash.

The bathroom door opened again and Roy, her waste of a boyfriend, strolled out, his towel wrapped around his waist. His mere presence made my skin crawl.

"Hey, Mel, how you doing?" he said, looking me up and down like he always did. While Jeanine's minuscule living room was fine when it was just the two of us, whenever Roy was here it felt like the walls were closing in. And every time Roy looked at me it turned my stomach. I didn't want to say anything to Jeanine. She was head over heels for Roy, but he gave me the creeps. There was more than one occasion when I woke up on the couch to catch him staring at me, pretending he was just on his way to the bathroom. It's not like I could ask her not to invite him over. It was her place, not mine. I was the interloper here. Always the person on the outside, just trying to fit in or make myself as invisible as possible.

"Fine, Roy," I said through gritted teeth, trying to sound pleasant. "The little girl was Rhys Thayer's daughter. He came in a while after you left," I said to Jeanine, trying my best to ignore her gag-reflex-inducing boyfriend.

"Shut up," she screeched, throwing her towel at me. I had to laugh. Jeanine certainly had a flair for the dramatic. Hence her weekly auditions for Broadway shows and musicals. It hadn't worked out so far, but I hoped someday she'd get her break. "What was he like?" she asked, pulling me down onto the couch. *How to describe him?* His deep chestnut eyes, light brown hair, and voice that sent shivers down my spine, even now, were hard to put into words that didn't make me sound like a fangirl. The way he looked at me, it made me twist and squirm in my seat.

"He was nice. Relieved to have found his daughter. He said his people would be in touch with me about some papers or something they need me to sign."

"Maybe he's giving you a reward," Roy said, intruding as ever, chugging my orange juice, the one with my name written on it, directly out of the carton before wiping his mouth with the back of his hand. I bit my tongue.

"I'm sure he's not. I didn't do anything. She found me," I said, turning back to Jeanine.

"I've seen him on the cover of a bunch of magazines and that big campaign he did last month to raise money for wells in Africa. He seems so nice," she said, bouncing. He did seem nice in all those interviews and articles I'd seen over the years. But our interaction hadn't been like that. It was different. Made me feel different. It hadn't made me feel like I was in the presence of one of the world's youngest billionaires, most generous benefactors and eligible bachelors.

My stomach had knotted like I'd been called into the principal's office for doing nothing wrong. He'd sized me up, scrutinizing me, trying to figure me out. And I didn't know if I wanted him to. As screwed up as my life was, he'd probably press charges against me for trying to steal his kid.

5

RHYS

Melanie Bright. Her name stuck in my mind, along with the rest of her, as I replayed our run-in at the diner. She'd kept Esme safe, and taken care of her after she ran off. That should have been the end of it. But I couldn't get her out of my mind. The scenes replaying in my head were driving me insane. I was not a man who fawned over a woman. I wasn't a man who bought flowers and chocolates and showed up with a limo. The world thought I was the perfect bachelor, rich, good looking, widowed, but really, I was just a fucked up guy who didn't want to go down the path of marriage again. I couldn't let someone have control over my actions, my thoughts, or my heart, which was why Melanie Bright pissed me off.

Derek walked in with a handful of files in his hand.

"I've got the files of the agencies applicants. I took the liberty of going through them myself and narrowing it down to these five." He held the folders out to me.

"No," I said, shaking my head. It wouldn't work.

"Take a look at them. There are some really good guys in

here. There's even one woman. Ex-military, excellent references."

"No." I crossed my arms across my chest and stared at him. He went into statue sentry mode, which he did whenever he was nervous. "You. That's who Esme needs."

"Thayer, we've been over this."

"We have and I don't know why you think it won't work. She likes you." I rounded my desk and grabbed a glass from the bar cart. The silver and glass clinked as I poured two drinks. The amber liquor sloshed into the tumbler and I held out one of the glasses to Derek.

"Come on." I motioned to the glass.

"I'm on the clock," he said, his arms plastered across his chest.

"And I'm the boss. Have a drink." Derek relented and took the glass from my hand. I took a sip, letting the oaky flavor burn its way down my throat.

"Why don't you think you can do it?"

"She's a little girl. She doesn't need someone like me towering over her like a walking nightmare." He gulped down half his drink. For some reason, Derek thought he was a bad guy. I had no idea why. His professionalism was unmatched. His recommendations were all top-notch, and he'd never missed a day of work. Plus, he hadn't let my six-year-old wander out into the city streets on her own.

"After what happened at the bank and the diner, there's no one I trust more."

"She doesn't like me. She doesn't even talk to me," he said, swirling his drink in the crystal tumbler.

"It's nothing personal, Derek. She doesn't talk to anyone, except for me."

"And Melanie…" Derek let that hang in the air between

us. He took a sip of his drink, enjoying my discomfort at the mention of her. And Melanie.

Melanie's presence in my head unsettled me. I didn't like it and I'd have to excise her from my mind. The only issue was Esme. She liked her. She'd asked for her a few times already. Maybe I could wait her out. Wait for her to forget about the waitress with legs that didn't quit and a waist I wouldn't mind wrapping my hands around. And there she was again, invading my head. I flung myself back from my desk and ran my hands through my hair. This did not bode well for me. I needed to focus. I didn't need any distractions right now.

"What do you think about her?"

"Her file checks out. She was nice and Esme talked to her. I'd say that's about as close as you can get to perfect," he said, draining his glass.

There was a gentle knock on the door. Derek swung it open and Rachel stood in the doorway. Her arms full of binders and her tablet balanced precariously on top. Her hair flew every which way. She was a fairly new assistant to me. Her father asked me to do him a favor, but she didn't need to know that. I knew the things a dad needed to do to make his daughter happy, so I went along with it. Plus, he promised me his vote for all my upcoming charity board elections.

Derek plucked the binders from her arms and put them on the solid oak desk. My father's desk. I hated that fucking thing. But something about being in the room, closed up kept me from losing my mind.

"Hi, Rachel." I drained the last of my drink.

"Hi, Mr. Thayer," she said, out of breath. I shot her a look. "I mean Rhys. Sorry." Her cheeks turned a bright shade of pink. Mr. Thayer was my father.

"I wanted to bring over your files for the meetings this week." She stacked the binders in two neat piles in front of my chair. I flipped through some of the papers. One week's worth of meetings.

Serving on the boards meant Esme and I could maintain a certain lifestyle. My little girl deserved the very best. The terms of my parents' will were draconian, but I'd make sure she never had to deal with anything like that. She'd never question how truly loved she was. Never doubted how much I cared about her and I lost my shit when she went missing. It wasn't like her. She didn't wander. She didn't even talk, at least she didn't before.

"Is there anything else you need me for?" Rachel politely asked, her hands clasped in front of her. I glanced outside; the sun had set ages ago.

"No, sorry, Rachel. You can go." Rachel picked up her tablet and headed for the door. I sat at the desk. Derek followed her out.

"Derek, I'm not taking no for an answer on this one. Until we find someone better, you're her shadow." He gave me a grim nod before following Rachel out. With them both gone, my mind wandered back to Melanie.

She got Esme to speak. She'd changed something in my little girl. I'd noticed it immediately. Now Esme didn't shy away as much around other people. Her confidence, which had been nonexistent before, grew every day. Esme even reenacted her bit of heroics with Melanie's scrapes, using her stuffed animals as patients and rescuers.

Melanie had done something in a few hours that so many others, professionals in their fields, failed to accomplish. I didn't know if I could just walk away from that. I wanted to know more and it irritated me to no end.

Maybe I could just get her out of my system, fuck her

and move on, but I doubted it would work, especially if Esme wanted her around and felt connected with her. I didn't want to screw my kid up any more than I already had. I was stuck.

Fuck her and forget her wasn't going to work. And that shook me to my core. That was how I worked. How I made sure my encounters with women were on terms I dictated. It was how I'd survived in the years since my wife died. I didn't know if I could take a chance on Mel. My desire to rid myself of this infatuation might end up breaking all my rules.

The last woman I was with stormed out after I told her the score and what she could and couldn't do. If it weren't for the ironclad NDA, I'm sure that headline would have been splashed all over the papers. And there would be a slew of other ones to accompany it. I fuck a woman until I'm tired of her, and then throw her back into the sea of women just like her. I use them like they want to use me. If it weren't for my money, influence, and looks, I'm under no illusions that a woman would want anything to do with me. Hell, I don't even think my looks matter. I could have a horn growing out of my forehead and a woman would tell me how she's always wanted to ride a unicorn. I learned that lesson early, made the mistake once, and wasn't going to make it again.

I didn't waste my time thinking about one woman. I thought about women in the abstract. If I wanted a redhead, a brunette, a blonde. Maybe even a woman with rainbow hair or that gray look some chicks were doing.

But I hadn't had a single woman stuck in my head for a long time. It unsettled me. I chalked it up to her helping my daughter. A daughter no man ever better think about the way I thought about women.

The plans I'd spent years putting into place were coming together. I didn't need distractions. My full inheritance was only a few months away. I'd no longer be the marionette dancing on my dead parents' strings. But I had to continue to fulfill the terms of their will, and that meant wearing this mask just a bit longer. I'd bided my time this long, what're a few more months? Then I can finally have the life I deserve. A life no longer under the thumb of two people who didn't give a shit about me. They had their masks as well. Caring, doting parents in public, but in private, I don't think I saw them more than once a week.

6

RHYS

"Daddy, can I go see Mel today?" Esme waltzed into my room when the sun had barely crested above the horizon a few days after her runaway incident. I could barely pry my eyes open. I'd only managed to get to sleep a couple of hours before.

Esme asked this same question every day, multiple times a day since it happened. So much for hoping she'd forget. The orange glow cast long shadows over the city as I glanced out the floor-to-ceiling windows that ringed our fiftieth-floor apartment. I stretched my arms overhead and yawned.

"You didn't get to spend enough time with her before?" I patted the bed beside me.

"No, I want to see her again," she said, bouncing in place.

"Why, Esme?"

"I like her. She's pretty, she's nice, she gave me hot chocolate and I got to help fix her. She hurt herself and I gave her one of my hankies and I made it better. And then she took care of me." She flopped back on the bed and bounced her feet up and down.

I gathered her up in my arms. Every day, I marveled at how lucky I was to have her. When I looked at her, I saw the best of her mother. The things that were the first to go when her addiction took hold. Her kindness and openness.

Esme didn't ask for much, so when she did, it meant it was serious. It didn't make sense. I couldn't understand what it was about Melanie that Esme couldn't let go of. There were plenty of things about her that stood out to me, her eyes, her ass, her feisty attitude, but these were clearly not the same things that my daughter admired. I needed to figure this out before I moved forward with my plan, to ensure there wasn't something I missed.

"You've had plenty of people take care of you, Esme. Why do you want to see Melanie?"

"I want to see if her owie is better. She was bleeding and I saw her and it made me sad. I wanted to help her. I wanted to make her happy," Esme said, beaming and bouncing on my bed. I couldn't help but smile. I love this little girl. I love her more than I ever thought possible. And it looked like my do-gooder ways were rubbing off on her. "Maybe she could come here. I could show her my room."

"I think it's a great plan, Esme. I think that could be arranged." I needed something from Melanie and I'm sure we could come to an agreement. One way or another she would help us. She'd been able to crack through Esme's shell and I wasn't going to let her shrink back inside, not when there was so much at stake—for both of us.

My afternoon plans were thrown off by an urgent call from

Rachel. Documents had arrived from all the foundations of which I'm a board member. These were notifications of previously unannounced elections taking place at the end of the year. This didn't happen. It never happened. It was every organization I belonged to, which set off the warning bells in my head. Something was going on.

"Rachel, I need you to get to the bottom of this. Figure out what's going on and report back to me. I need to know who's behind this." I ended the call and stared out over the city, my hands shoved deep in my pockets. It was the place I'd called home for the past ten years. Home. The clouds on the horizon churned and brewed with something ominous and I needed to know what it was so I could put a stop to it. There was so much more at stake than money.

The massive amounts of money I threw at these organizations meant my seats had always been secure, until now. I closed myself up in my office, the familiar smells of wood and leather calmed me as I slid behind the desk I hated, and poured over the documents myself, looking for some indication of what might have pushed everyone to call these elections all at once. I knew who was behind it, but I still didn't understand why. Losing a seat would completely screw over the plans I had for Esme and myself.

The door swung open and Esme came barreling in with her coloring books and crayons in hand.

"Can I color, daddy?" The pages of her coloring book rustled as she laid down in front of the large windows, everything fanned out in front of her.

"Of course." Maybe I should just walk away from everything. Take her and go. No, I'd sacrificed so much already, I was at least going to make sure my little girl came out on the other end of this without a care in the world. She sat in the corner coloring as I flipped through folder after folder. She was perfectly content.

I needed to get out of this office, this building. In the breaks from worrying about what the loss of these seats might do, my mind drifted to Melanie.

"Hey Es, do you want to go see if Melanie is working right now?" I asked, standing up from my chair. Esme immediately perked up and ran to put on her coat. I grabbed the folders Rachel had delivered earlier off the desk. Now was the perfect time to let Melanie Bright know she would be working for me by the end of the day.

7

MEL

The smell of freshly baked cookies filled the air. Shannon had on her funny frog oven mitts. I loved it when she would talk to me in the funny voices with those puppets. But now my eyes were glued to the chocolate chip cookies that she pulled out of the oven.

"Back up, Mel. These are super hot." She set the baking sheet on the stove and grabbed the second tray.

"Can I have one now?" The smell was overpowering me. I wanted to gobble up every single one right away. My feet kicked back and forth in my chair at the kitchen table. My homework was spread out in front of me, along with a tall glass of milk. Carrots and grapes were in a little bowl. My brain food, Shannon called them.

"Not until after dinner. These are because you did such a great job at your violin recital." I'd been so nervous. I had only been playing for a few months, but the instructor said I was a natural.

"Please, can I have one now?" I put on my best dopey puppy face, sticking out my bottom lip. Shannon burst out laughing.

"Okay, fine, kiddo. But you better eat all your veggies at

dinner." She picked up one of the piping hot cookies off the tray and put it on a small plate in front of me. I loved her so much. I wrapped my arms around her waist and hugged her to me. She always smelled so good.

"I love you, Shannon."

"I love you too, kiddo," she said, rustling my hair.

I jolted awake, covered in sweat. My heart thundered in my chest. The same nightmare plagued me for years. I'd never been able to shake it. I glanced over and jumped.

Roy's knees were the first thing I saw. He sat on the coffee table, less than two feet away. Any other time, I'd roll over and pray he'd go away. It wasn't the first time I'd caught him watching me. But I couldn't afford to make waves.

I paid Jeanine a portion of the rent. I wasn't a freeloader, but I wasn't on the lease or anything. I couldn't roll over this time because he was so close. I didn't trust him. His cheap cologne filled my nose and made me want to puke. As my eyes adjusted, I saw his arm working up and down on his dick. His sweatpants were pulled down in the front and he stroked himself, staring right at me. I yelped and jumped up onto the couch. There was nowhere else for me to go. He was too close.

"What the fuck, Roy?" I bellowed. My heart pounded in my throat.

"Just lay back down, Mel. I'll be finished soon," he said, still palming his dick, like it was completely natural for him to be jerking off in front of me while I slept. My stomach turned and my fight-or-flight instincts went into high gear. It was the same nauseous dread I lived through so many nights growing up.

He leaned forward and, out of instinct, I hit him as hard as I could right in the nose. As much as I wanted to, I didn't knee him in the balls. He'd probably like that.

"You fucking bitch," he said, with his hands over his nose. Blood spilled out from between his fingers and I held my hands out ready in case he came after me.

"What the hell's going on out here?" Jeanine walked out of the bedroom and froze, taking it all in. I gulped air through my constricted throat.

"Jeanine, he—"

"Why the hell is your dick out, Roy?" she screeched.

"Jeanine. I was sleeping and when I woke up. Roy was sitting on the table with his dick in his hand."

"She's lying, babe." He finally took a step back from the couch and cupped his hand over his nose, blood covering his lips.

"What?" I shouted.

"I was just walking to the bathroom and she called me over to the couch." He took Jeanine's hand in his. She tried to tug it away, but he held onto her.

"That's a lie!" I got off the couch, my feet sticking to the peeling laminate flooring. He kept talking like I hadn't said a word.

"She said she had something to tell me, and told me to sit on the table. I did and she stuck her hands down my pants and pulled my dick out, babe. I swear."

"You're a fucking liar, Roy. I would never, Jeanine. I would never," I said vehemently.

"You know how she's always been. When I told her, no way, that you're my girl and I don't want anyone else, she punched me in the nose."

Angry tears prickled in my eyes. Jeanine looked from him to me.

"You know I love you," he said, laying it on thick, and I saw the moment she decided she'd rather believe the lie than face the truth. She reached up to cup his face in her hands.

"Are you okay, babe? Let me get you some ice." She skirted around him and got some ice from the freezer. She avoided my gaze the entire time. I rushed into the bathroom and didn't come out until Roy's heavy footfalls thundered across the floor and the door slammed. He was gone.

I came out of the bathroom. Jeanine leaned against the kitchen counter, holding her coffee mug and staring off into space. She glanced over at me. Her reddened eyes tracked me as I grabbed some clothes out of my bag. I didn't know what to do. *What do I say? I told her that her boyfriend was a total creeper. What was left?* I knew all about what happens when you tell a woman who doesn't want to hear it that her boyfriend came on to you. It doesn't turn out well.

We worked different shifts that day and the next, and I'd been on an apartment hunt every spare minute I had. I didn't have any money for a deposit. My account had been drained. I needed to go to the bank and open a new account. The promises I'd been given that the money in there wouldn't be touched without my permission were obviously worth nothing.

Every apartment I found was way out of my price range or filled with creepers. Weren't there any decent people left in the city who didn't need an arm and a leg as a deposit?

8

MEL

"Hey, Mel. Can I talk to you?" Jeanine pulled me aside by our lockers and fidgeted with the hem of her off-white apron, picking at the stray threads around the edges. Her chipped red nails caught my eye with each flick back and forth. She was nervous and her nervousness twisted my gut.

"Morning, Jeanine," I said, trying to keep my voice as level as possible.

"I thought I could put what you did behind me," she said, clutching the mug in her hands. I closed my eyes, my pulse pounded and my hands shook. "It's okay. I know what a catch Roy is. But he's not going to stray, Mel. And your throwing yourself at him—" My brain did a stutter step. *Throwing myself at him? After what I told her? After what she saw?*

Shame crawled all over me, souring my stomach. I hung my head. "I'm going to need you to leave soon," she said, not even looking the least bit angry. That told me all I needed to know. She knew it was a lie. She'd worked through every possible scenario as to why it wasn't him. Why it was her fault because she couldn't keep him happy. Why it was my fault for coming on to him or existing in the first place. I'd seen it all before, and I knew no matter what I had to say in my defense, I might as well say it to a brick wall. She wouldn't see until she was ready, if ever. It had been good while it lasted, but now it was time for me to go.

"Mel, did you hear me? I said I need you out today." Thud. It hit me so hard I staggered back a step. *Today*. I know she said soon, but I thought she'd at least give me a week. I willed the tears that prickled the back of my eyes not to form. By sheer will, I choked them back.

"Roy has to be out of his apartment and, well, I think this is a really great step for us in the right direction. I think it means he's finally getting serious," she said hopefully. It took everything in me not to scream in her face about what an idiot she was. I fisted my hands at my side.

"Can I at least leave my stuff in the apartment for a bit?" I asked, running my hands through my hair. Shelters weren't exactly safe places to have your belongings, no matter how meager they might be.

"I don't think that would be a good idea. I brought your duffle with me. It's next to your locker."

I closed my eyes and tilted my chin up at the ceiling. *Take a breath. Take a breath*. I repeated the mantra. This was why I didn't let people get close. It only ended in disappointment and pain. How fucking sad was it that everything I owned could be shoved into a duffle bag and dropped off anywhere? Here I thought Jeanine was kind of a friend, her horrible taste in men aside. She was pretty much the only friend I had in the whole city, not that that said much.

"Back to work, ladies. I don't pay you to yap," Martin called, leaning out of his office door. I unballed my fists and brushed past Jeanine. She called out what sounded like an apology from behind me, but I just kept going. I needed this job and I didn't need to get fired for knocking out a co-worker. I stomped over to my newest table, repeating my mantra again. *Breathe.* I opened my eyes at the same time a small body slammed into me, tiny arms wrapping around my waist.

"Mel!" Esme said, bouncing up and down in front of me. The tight ball in my chest unfurled a little. Her enthusiasm was exactly what I needed right now.

The kid could put a smile on anyone's face. I couldn't say I hadn't thought about her since the day I found her—well, she found me. And I peered into the booth at the other person who'd run through my mind more times than I could count since that day. Someone had come into the diner for me to sign a bunch of NDA stuff, but other than that I hadn't heard from him since.

Rhys stared at me with a look I couldn't quite place. *Breathe.* When he looked at me like that it set my skin aflame. A scarlet flush traveled up my neck. *Get it together.*

"Hello, Ms. Bright," he said, his voice pouring over me like honey, and his eyes boring into mine. The way he said my name, it almost felt like a dirty word. A word you shouldn't say in public, let alone in front of a child. Much better said with my legs wrapped around his head. *Okay, down, girl.*

What little research I'd done on him, let me know it was in my mind. Every picture I saw of him had a model, actress or powerful woman on his arm. This was a man who commanded audiences with heads of states and royalty. The women on his arm at events ranged from supermodels to movie stars. He wasn't here for anything more than humoring Esme.

"I signed all the papers you needed me to. I'd never tell

anyone about what happened. Kids wander off. It happens," I said, shrugging my shoulders.

"Yes, I know you signed the papers and I appreciate your discretion," he said, his cool green eyes boring into mine. His words wrapped their way around me, weaving their way up and down my spine. "It's always difficult to find people who are willing to do the right thing and not take advantage of a situation," he said. His voice entranced me and all his words seemed to have more meaning behind them.

He was trouble. Trouble for someone like me who didn't know anything about a man like him, and who wasn't brave enough to try to tread water in the deep end where he lived. The waves he made were more likely to drown me than any man I'd ever been around before. Not that there had been an invitation. I'm not in his league. I cleared my throat and my mind.

"What can I get you two?" I asked, dropping my eyes to my note pad. Esme tugged me down to her level. I crouched and she cupped her hands around my ear.

"Hot chocolate," Esme whispered, sliding back into the booth and grinning up at me. She had on another cute ensemble that probably cost more than a month's rent. I couldn't help but return her smile. This kid had an infectious energy.

"And for you," I asked, taking a breath and looking at him again.

"I'll have the same," he said, handing the menu back to me. My hand gently brushed his and I nearly dropped the menus. I needed to get it together. *Stop losing it over a guy who's not thinking twice about you.*

"Excellent, two hot chocolates coming up." I left their table and got their drinks. A late breakfast crowd poured in not long after and things picked up for a while. I got them another couple of mugs of hot chocolate before they left. Disappointment panged in my gut that I hadn't been able to talk to them a little more, but other tables beckoned and I needed the tips. I really needed the tips.

I spent my entire shift trying not to think about what the hell I was going to do tonight after my shift. Maybe I could convince Martin to let me work a double. Unlikely, as the overnight crew was territorial about their late-night regulars. A hotel, even a hostel was way out of my price range right now. I wanted to wrap my hands around Colleen's neck and strangle her for stealing from me. But that meant I'd have to be in the same room with her, and I'd managed to avoid that for nearly five years.

I didn't know if I'd be able to get into a shelter tonight. They usually filled up early. I collected the tip from my last table and checked the time. Maybe I'd be able to swing it if I headed out now. I ran to my locker, grabbed some stuff and decided I'd be better off leaving my duffle there. At least it would be safe for tonight. I burst out the back door into the alley and skidded to a stop when I saw a dark figure leaning up against the brick wall right across from the door.

My heart thudded in my chest, fear flooded my body and then I looked closer. *Rhys*. He looked so completely out of place in the dingy alley, in his long, probably cashmere navy coat and gloves. He was so shiny and new, I swore I could smell his freshly laundered clothes from here, even with the dumpster less than five feet away. And as out of place as he looked, he seemed completely at ease, like his evenings were often spent hanging out in alleys behind diners, waiting for waitresses to get off their shifts.

But I didn't have time for him right now. The complications in my life quickly turning my simmering headache into a throbbing one. I needed to keep my feet firmly on the ground, and right now I needed to get to the women's shelter and see if they might have a bed available for me. *How's that for some reality?*

"Ms. Bright, I was wondering if I would have to come in there after you," he said, pushing off the wall. His movements were purposeful and calculated. I wondered if there was anything in his life he didn't have complete control over. Then what he said, sunk in and I scrunched my eyebrows trying to figure out why he'd waited out here for me at all.

"I'm not sure why. My shift only ended five minutes ago and I am kind of in a rush. If you need me to sign some more papers or something, you can have someone drop them by the diner and I'll sign them tomorrow," I said, taking off toward the street.

"I'm not here about any other papers." He trailed behind me. His footsteps echoed off the walls of the alley.

"I don't have time for small talk. I need to get to my train," I said, trying to shake him. I was going someplace he'd probably never been, unless it was for a photo op for a donation or something. The shame and anger burned in my gut that I'd be spending the night in a shelter or on a bench.

"No problem, I'll walk with you," he said, falling in step beside me and sliding his hands into his pockets.

"It's okay. I'll be fine. I'm just heading to the train." *Please leave me alone, so I can beg for a bed without you watching.*

"I insist," he said. His tone brokered no argument. I zipped my coat and kept walking. The shelter was ten blocks from here, but I wasn't going to tell him that. I'd promised myself the last time I was in a shelter that I wasn't going back. Life sure had a way of kicking me in the fucking teeth. I gripped the strap of my bag as I hustled down the street, Rhys right beside me. Usually, I seemed to get knocked into by every single person in my path. With him, the world took notice and moved out of the way as he stepped forward to walk ahead of me.

He had his own gravitational pull that forced people to bend to his will, whether they noticed it or not. Noticing the crowd didn't have the same aversion to jostling me, he put his hand on my elbow and guided me through the people. Obviously, his power worked by proxy and I was safe in his bubble. People didn't dare bump into or jostle those in the bubble. Even through my jacket, I felt the heat of his touch on my skin. I didn't know if it was real or imagined, but it made my knees a little wobbly as we wove our way through the streets.

"Esme really likes you, Melanie," he said, keeping his eyes straight ahead. It was the first time he'd said my first name and it sent a shiver down my spine.

"I like her, too. She's a good kid. I hope she didn't get into too much trouble for wandering off," I said, glancing over at him. He had amazingly long and thick eyelashes. I found myself staring at them, observing him in the wild. Out on the streets like a normal person, but he was anything but normal.

"She didn't get into too much trouble, but she knows not to repeat it. Which station?" he said, glancing over at me. I stumbled. *Shit.* I needed a station.

"33rd. I'm heading to 33rd." He nodded and took the next right. I sped up to keep pace with him. He seemed to notice and slowed his gait.

"I have a proposition for you, Melanie," he said as we walked. The word proposition did all kinds of crazy crap to my stomach.

"Esme is quite taken with you. She enjoys your company

and you have her talking, which makes you a miracle worker in my book. I'd like you to come work for me as her nanny." I stumbled again.

"Her nanny," I squeaked. I barely liked kids, I didn't think I should be in charge of the wellbeing of one. I mean, I was nice to them and was okay being around them for short periods of time, but I wasn't nanny material. My bag was not filled with gumdrops and rainbows. It had some crumpled one-dollar bills, old gum wrappers and every bobby pin that had ever been in my hair. Not a single musical number or umbrella to be found.

"Yes, I think you could be good for her."

What really stopped me cold about the whole thing was the thought of a background check. It soured my stomach and made my palms sweaty. He'd absolutely run a check on me, if I came to work for him. And probably not just a standard one, but a crazy in-depth one that would tell him every cavity I'd ever had. I didn't need that kind of poking and prodding into my past. I didn't let myself think too hard about my past on most days.

"I don't think that would be a good idea. I'm not really good with kids."

"You're good with Esme and that's all I care about," he said, like it was an open and shut case, and it probably was to him. I couldn't imagine what it would be like to go through life with so much certainty. I didn't even know where I would be getting my next meal. Well, it would probably be the diner, but other than that, my life was up in the air. I knew there were some things that were certain in this world, but I knew they were far outside my reach.

"Rhys, Mr. Thayer, I don't think it would be a good idea. I'm sure there are tons of people who would be a better fit to be Esme's nanny."

9

RHYS

She didn't want to take the job. Perhaps it should provide me a bit of solace to know she wasn't jumping at the chance to become Esme's nanny. To me, it meant she wasn't a user. Most people saw an opportunity like this as a chance to bilk me out of as much money as they could. Melanie walked beside me, wearing a purple coat that didn't look anywhere near thick enough for the plummeting temperatures. It was on its last legs. She needed a new coat and she needed it now. I made a mental note to have Rachel arrange for one to be sent to her room. She didn't know it yet, but she wasn't going to turn me down. I wouldn't give her the choice.

"I think you should find someone else. I have a lot of stuff going on in my life right now and I don't want to burden you with my trivial issues," she said, taking her elbow out of my hand. I glanced down at my empty hand and back at her. I shoved my gloved hand back into my pocket, her warmth gone. "I really appreciate the offer. I do. But I think you're going to need to find someone else."

She bolted for the station entrance. I watched her scurry

down the stairs to the station. I wasn't quite sure what to think of her at that point. I'd read her file. I knew her background and someone like her should have jumped at the chance. But she turned me down. Whether she realized it or not, she'd turned it into a game. I always enjoyed a good game, and knew this was one I'd be sure to win.

Derek pulled the SUV up to the curb. He'd tailed us on our little walk since Esme was back in the apartment with Rachel. As I closed the car door, I caught a flash of electric purple coming up the station stairs. *Melanie.* She glanced around and hurried off in the opposite direction.

"Follow her." Derek pulled into traffic and the slow progress made it easy to follow her as she wove her way through the salted and snow-slicked streets. The crowds had thinned out since we'd left the diner, and the people on the streets had transitioned from starry-eyed tourists to hollow-faced addicts. I shook my head. I hadn't thought I could be so wrong about Melanie. Disappointment hit me that I'd been so far off the mark when it came to her. It wasn't until she darted inside a large converted church that I wondered if my assumptions about her were wrong yet again. A faded sign hung over the door, "Women's Mission Coalition." *Did she volunteer here?* She hadn't come to score, she'd come to help.

I hopped out of the SUV and strode inside. The stagnant smell of stale coffee, bleach, and floral air freshener packed a pungent punch as the door closed behind me.

"Do you have any beds for the night?" Melanie asked the woman behind the scratched and scuffed Plexiglas.

"I don't think so, hun," she said. Melanie hung her head, her shoulders slumping. "But let me check." I stood there completely stunned, my feet glued to the ground. She wasn't here to help, she was here for a place to stay. Waitresses didn't make much, but she shouldn't have to go to a homeless shelter. My mind wandered to all the things that could happen to a person down on her luck without a place to stay in the city. Blood pounded through my veins and my fingers tingled. I fisted them at my sides. She didn't even entertain the offer to work for me. She'd brushed me off without a second thought. She'd rather spend her nights in a homeless shelter than with me?

"Melanie, what the hell are you doing here?" I said, louder than I intended, my anger getting the best of me. Melanie jumped at the sound of my voice, as both women whipped their heads around toward me. Melanie's mouth opened and closed like a fish. The color drained out of her face as she stared back, her eyes wide.

"I...I..." she stuttered, grasping for the words to explain what the hell was going on.

"I'll donate one hundred thousand dollars to the shelter if you don't give her a bed for tonight," I said, reaching for my wallet.

"What the hell are you doing here? How did you know I was here?" she asked, snapping out of her shocked silence.

"I followed you," I said, waiting for her reaction. Her eyes got comically wide and she gripped onto the strap of her bag with both hands.

"Why would you do that?" she asked through gritted teeth.

A loud buzzer went off, and the woman behind the counter opened the door beside her desk.

"Do you need to come in, sweetheart? Come on in. We'll find something for you," she said, motioning for Melanie to join her on the other side of the door. On the other side, safely tucked away from me.

"Should I be offended, Melanie? You'd rather spend the

night in a homeless shelter than with my daughter and me? A nice warm bed in your own room. Safe and sound," I said, advancing on her. She stood rooted to the spot, her eyes pinned on me.

"Melanie, honey, come inside," the woman said, holding the door open and taking a step out.

"Three hundred thousand, if you don't give her a bed for the night," I said, keeping my eyes on Melanie. She sucked in a breath, her eyes bouncing from me to the woman.

"You can't buy us off, and we're not going to turn someone away who's being threatened. Melanie, come in. He can't get to you in here."

"Miss, I don't know what it is about me that might have screamed abusive boyfriend or husband, but I can assure you it's not the case. I'm simply a potential employer for Melanie and I'm a bit shocked she didn't let me know how dire her situation was. I'd have easily solved this little problem of hers," I said, staring at Melanie, who averted her eyes. She ducked her head and her shoulders rounded as she folded her arms around herself. *Shame.* I knew it well. It burned in me so many times over the years, but I didn't like the way it looked on her.

"Why don't you tell her, Melanie?" I said, sure the woman had called the police on me before stepping out into the doorway. Melanie glanced up at me again and back at the woman.

"He's not my boyfriend or anything. He's not a threat. I —" she gulped. She took a breath, closing her eyes. "I was embarrassed. And I'm pretty sure he's good for the donation, too, so I would make sure I got his info. I'm sure it could do a lot of good here," she said, forcing a smile and glancing around at the peeling paint and tattered chairs in the lobby.

"I'll just go," she said, trying to skirt around me. And that was the final straw. I was done being Mr. Nice Guy. My mask slipped and it was all her fault. I grabbed her elbow as she tried to pass by me. Not as her friendly neighborhood escort, but as a man who wasn't going to let her get away.

"Don't even think of walking away from me, Melanie. If you do, I have half the mind to put you over my knee and show you just how serious I am," I said, my mouth a hairsbreadth away from her ear. I felt the tremble race through her, but when I looked in her eyes, it wasn't fear I saw, it was something that made me want to push her up against the nearest wall and show her how serious I was. This woman toyed with me and I didn't even think she knew she was doing it. The power shifted somehow and now I was left grasping at what remained.

"You are not going to walk off into the cold night when I know you've just been visiting a homeless shelter, so you obviously have no place to go. You're coming home with me. Now." There was no argument here. I slid the mask back and turned to the woman in the doorway.

"Thanks so much for being so helpful to Melanie. I truly appreciate it and I'll be sure to have that donation check sent over first thing tomorrow." My plastic smile slid on as naturally as it ever had. It was second nature by now. When in doubt, smile in a wide toothy grin like a fucking idiot. I was aware of the effect I had on women. A hint of a smile tugged on the corners of the woman's lips. I kept my grip on Melanie's elbow in case she tried to bolt.

"Tell the woman thank you, Melanie," I said into her ear. She shivered again and I knew she didn't want to cause a scene. Didn't want to draw more attention to herself. I'd use whatever tricks I needed to get her where I wanted her. How I wanted her.

The woman in the doorway crossed her arms over her chest and I opened the door, the frigid air blasting us. We stepped out onto the street, and Melanie glanced over her shoulder at the woman.

"I'm fine, really and you know what, I think Mr. Thayer is feeling extra generous tonight, so why not double that donation," she said, smirking up at me. Cheeky, very cheeky. I waved to the woman and she waved back, dumbstruck. I kept my hand on Melanie, and the door slammed behind us as we went down the stairs, which were bathed in strobing blue and red lights. Derek spoke with the two squad cars that pulled up while we were inside. I gave the officers a wave and they eagerly waved back.

"What the hell was that?" she said, ripping her elbow out of my grip, and rounding on me.

"Get in the car, Melanie," I said, advancing on her. She took a step back, her hands clenched around the strap of her bag. She looked pissed. I relished her anger, her venom. She'd seen my mask falter and hadn't run away, but I didn't know how she'd react if she got more than a peek.

10

MEL

He was insane. Not eccentric. Not unconventional. He was fucking insane. Who gives away money like that, just so someone doesn't lend me a bed to sleep in? A bed that probably wasn't even available. I kept running over it in my head, and it didn't make sense. There was only one conclusion.

Rhys Thayer had lost his mind. I'd decided that during the car ride across town and cemented it in my mind as we rode up in the elevator to his penthouse apartment. The elevator only had one button. PH. This elevator was nicer than most places I'd slept over the past year. The warm wood and brass covered the entire thing floor to ceiling. There was even a mini chandelier hanging overhead.

I wondered if I could just camp out in there overnight. Being in the confined space with him wreaked havoc on me. Rhys stood perfectly still, but reminded me of a caged animal. Power poured off him in waves as he tapped away on his phone like I wasn't there. Like he hadn't stalked me to get me here.

After what felt like centuries, the elevator doors slid

open and he stepped out, leaving me plastered against the back of the elevator. The brass handrail warming up under the death grip I had on it. But I didn't have much of a choice about where to go. I knew the shelter proposition wasn't going to fly and I really didn't want to have to find a random place to sleep, so a penthouse wasn't the worst place to end up tonight. I didn't know exactly what Rhys had in mind. He seemed pretty adamant about my coming. *Was this just for Esme?*

"Don't make me come in there and get you, Melanie," he said, as he shook his coat off and laid it across the table by the door. I tentatively stepped out, my white-knuckled hands wrapped around the strap of my bag. I still didn't know what I was doing here. Well, other than the fact that I would have had to sleep on a park bench tonight, if I hadn't come with him, and the fact that he didn't seem inclined to let me go. The hulking security guy stood beside the couch.

The patter of small feet came down the hallway and Esme launched herself into the room and wrapped her arms around me for the second time that day.

"You came!" she said, her face buried in my stomach. "Daddy said you'd be coming over today. I'm so happy!" I threw a glance over my shoulder and Rhys quirked his eyebrow at me, as if to say, he was right, wasn't he? *Did anyone ever tell him 'no'?* Lord knows I'd tried.

"Hey, Esme. How was your day, kiddo?" I asked, crouching down in front of her and tousling her hair.

"Good, really good now that you're here. Daddy said he'd be able to get you to come, but it was so late and I didn't believe him."

"Your dad can be pretty convincing when he wants to be, kiddo," I said, and Rhys chuckled before disappearing down the hall.

"Come see my room," she said, tugging me along.

"Only for a minute, Esme. You know you're supposed to be in bed. It's so late right now."

I spent a few minutes in Esme's room, with her showing me pretty much every toy a kid could ever ask for. Her room was bigger than Jeanine's apartment. It wasn't until she let out her third yawn and her blinks got slower that I suggested she get back in bed. I kept checking the doorway, and had even ventured out a few steps into the apartment to look for Rhys, but he'd disappeared.

Esme climbed into bed, a book under her arm, and I tucked her in. Faint memories from a time I'd tried to forget flittered through my mind as I sat on the edge of the bed and read her the bedtime story. As I turned the last page, her soft snores made me smile. She wore herself out.

"See, you're a natural," came a voice from behind me. I yelped, nearly throwing the book across the room, and glanced down at Esme. She didn't move a muscle. Rhys leaned against the doorway, shadowed by the darkened hallway. "Come with me, I'll show you to your room," he said, before disappearing back into the hall.

I stood up, unsure my knees would hold me, and followed him into the dark hall.

My room. A place for me. I wondered if the nightmares would follow me there.

How was I going to tell him I shouldn't stay? I couldn't stay. *Where else did I have to go?* Maybe just for a few nights, until I figured things out. As much as he thought I was a natural, I'd had to fight episodes of panic throughout the short visit I'd shared with Esme. She was so happy. So incredibly happy with everything in her room. She loved showing it to me. She didn't have a care in the world, and my heart ached for all the kids out there like me growing up, kids who would never know this level of peace, comfort, and ease. She had more at six than I'd ever had in my entire life, except for the one year that still haunted me. It made things easier that way. Better to pretend it never happened than be crushed that it had.

Even with that jab in my gut, and pang in my chest, watching her in her own little world prancing, dancing and laughing, so happy made me smile. I pushed away my own pain and reveled in her joy. She was a great kid. A kid who deserved a lot better than me looking after her. But I didn't know how to convince her father of that.

I trailed behind Rhys, his muted steps reverberated through me like anvils dropping. His pull made me want to lean into him, speed up my steps, until I could breathe him in. The other part of me wanted to make a run for it and never look back. I could tell he wasn't a forgiving man and I was bound to disappoint.

He led me through a couple of turns before he opened the door in front of him and flicked on the lights. My breath caught as I stared past him into the room. The plush cream carpet looked soft enough to sleep on. There was an oversized reading chair next to the window in the corner, piled with green and blue pillows.

The floor-to-ceiling windows showcased the entire city, like a moving picture frame. And there was a new coat laying across the bed. It was purple like mine, but that was where the similarities ended. Everything about it screamed elegant, warm and comfortable.

He pushed the door open wider and motioned me inside. Cautiously, I poked my head inside. Rhys didn't move, so I brushed against him as I made my way past. Every cell in my body was completely aware of every point of contact our bodies made. His freshly laundered smell hung in the air as I passed through his wake. I made it to the other side, nearly gasping for air, but I couldn't push down the temptation to look back. When I did, he was so close our lips almost touched. The heat from his body against my back caused me to shiver as he spoke.

"This room comes with the job. It's not much, but I hope it will do," he said. His minty breath caressed my ear. The heavy, foreboding press of his body against mine made me wonder if I'd ever been around a man before. He was a man unlike any I'd ever encountered, and I didn't think I'd ever encounter anyone like him again. The pulsing pounding raced through my body like nothing I'd ever experienced. He hadn't even touched me, not really, and I was already addicted. I wanted him to touch me. I wanted his hands on my body, running across my skin, tickling the flesh between my thighs.

I bit my lip and put my hand against the wall to steady myself and took a step away. His heady presence was enough to make me forget everything that had ever worried me. Make me forget anything but the two of us in this room. Him standing so close to me, his eyes boring into me, devouring me. It was so easy to forget who I was outside of these walls when he looked at me like that. I couldn't afford to forget. Things like this didn't happen to me. Nothing good ever happened without me smashing back to earth more bruised and battered than before. I'd already had enough damage to last me a lifetime.

"I brought your bag in. Come with me and I'll show you the rest of the apartment." He slipped out of the room and I felt like I could breathe again. I was torn between locking the door until morning and following him wherever he wanted to take me. But that didn't seem like a request and I had no doubt he'd be coming after me if I didn't comply.

"Here's the gym." He pointed through the half glass door. A treadmill, free weights, a few weight machines and other standard gym equipment was lined up neatly against the mirrored wall. I'd almost walked past when a dancing blue light caught my eye.

"There's a pool?" I whirled around. My eyes must have been as big as saucers. He chuckled. The sound made me smile wide.

"There is a pool. Do you want to see it?" He pushed the door open. I wasn't even going to try to play it cool.

∽

I sat on the edge of the pool with my pants rolled up and my feet dangling in the water, staring at the lights of the city.

"The apartment certainly has its perks," he said from behind me, his hands shoved in his pockets. I couldn't have imagined a place like this existed high above everything going on down in the grime of the city. The floor-to-ceiling windows wrapped around the whole apartment. I was a bird perched on a ledge outside, watching everything pass by. It certainly made the city feel a whole lot calmer. Like anyone up here was the master of their domain. Maybe that was why Rhys came across that way, so in control of everything. When you were staring down at the city street watching everyone scrambling from your tranquil perch, how could you not feel like you owned everything as far as you could see?

"Ready to continue the tour?" He held a big fluffy towel out to me. I grabbed it and dried my feet. I'd forgotten I still hadn't seen the whole place.

Everything in the apartment fought for my attention. There were lamps with stained glass lampshades. The bookshelves were filled with leather bound books, I imagined cost more than I could make in a lifetime. The artwork on the walls looked like it belonged in a museum, and when I read some of the nameplates below a few of the frames, I saw I wasn't far off. On loan from the MET. *Who the hell could just borrow something from the Metropolitan Museum of Art?* Rhys Thayer, that's who. Every room held something unlike anything I'd ever seen, and the most intriguing of them all was Rhys himself.

Every glance, every brushed touch, every word had me on edge. The heat behind his gaze should have sent me running from the room, but it didn't. It wasn't like the leering of someone like Roy. Rhys stared at me like he wanted to possess me, not use me. His gaze held the promise of things I'd never experienced before, and my mouth watered to try them all. I had never had someone look at me like that. Like I was someone they couldn't wait to get their hands on. Like someone they needed to be close to.

I just didn't know how long it would last. *Was I just a passing infatuation? Did he sleep with all the other nannies? Look at them like he looked at me?* I wouldn't believe that I was someone so special that it made him sit up and take notice. So why did I want to be near him when he had the power to destroy me with a word. I guess I hadn't yet learned my lesson about flying too close to the sun.

I'd been programmed to be hurt. People don't last, and he's so far out of my league it's not even comprehensible. Regardless, if I wanted to do this job right, I shouldn't start it out by sleeping with my boss. But the temptation was real and raw, pounding in my chest like a signal drum of impending war. A war of the wills, and I wasn't sure I was strong enough to win.

We finished the tour when he showed me to the kitchen.

"Wine?" he said, moving behind the counter.

"Sure," I said, following him.

"No, have a seat," he said, gesturing to the living room.

I watched him in the reflection in the glass, the city lights surrounding him, making him seem even more like a mirage. He moved efficiently around the kitchen, opening, and closing cabinets and drawers. He knew where everything was. I imagined he'd have a staff crawling all over this place, taking care of his every whim but other than the guy who drove us to the building, I hadn't seen anyone else in the apartment. Every so often he caught my eye in the reflection and held me pinned there, in his skin-tingling gaze, until he decided to break the connection. His choice, every time. Each time he looked away I had to remember to breathe again. Remember my name. His gaze lingered, and it was like a fiery embrace wrapped around me, my skin singed by his vision.

"Here you go," he said, holding out a glass of chardonnay. He hadn't even asked what I liked. *How did he know I hated red?* My hand wrapped around the cool, smooth glass, momentarily brushing against his, and that energy that pulsed between us remained unspoken, but I knew he felt it.

I turned and mumbled a "Thank you." *Keep it together, Mel. Keep it together.*

"What do you think?" he asked, walking over to the couches and sitting, stretching long legs out in front of him, and his arm out over the back. He was sin, wrapped in a mixture of masculinity and refinement. *How many other women found themselves treading water in the wake of his power?*

"This place is amazing," I said, taking a gulp of my wine and sitting in a chair across from him. My leg nervously bounced up and down and some of the wine sloshed onto my hand.

"It serves its purpose. And about the job? You start tonight." he said, his eyes on me as he tipped his crystal tumbler back, sipping the dark amber liquid inside.

"I...I still think you're making a mistake. I don't think I'm going to be able to give Esme what she needs," I said, apparently trying to talk myself into homelessness. The urge to say *yes* sat on the tip of my tongue, but every time I looked at him I forgot my name, forgot to breathe, and forgot how to talk. And I knew this would send me down a path from which, I might never recover, a path where the world was spread out for me on a platter and then snatched away. I knew where I'd end up. More bruised, battered and even more shattered than when I started.

"Esme has the best teachers, tutors and other specialists she could ever need. What she doesn't have is someone she feels comfortable enough to talk to, and be as free with as I've seen her be with you. For now, that's all she needs," he said, leaning forward.

"There are some things in my past," I said, taking a sip of wine.

"I know. I've already read your file. There's nothing in there that concerns me."

"But—" I said, trying to decide how I felt about that. He'd already had me researched, dissected, and analyzed. It made sense, a man like him didn't make an offer like his, to come live in his house, without vetting someone first. I wondered how deep that research went. *Did he know everything about my past?*

"There is nothing in there that concerns me, Melanie. Don't worry so much. And I took the liberty of calling the diner. You won't be going back there," he said, taking another drink like he hadn't just taken away the steadiest thing I had in my life.

"What the hell? I didn't say I'd take the job. I didn't say I wanted to quit the diner," I said, jumping up. It wasn't his place to interfere in my life like that.

"You didn't have to. It's not like you'll have the time, if you're going to be with Esme." I took a deep breath. It was a shitty job, but it was still the only job I had. I rubbed my hand against my temple. This was insane. He was insane. Swirling his drink around in his glass like he didn't have a care in the world, and he didn't, did he? He held the power, and I was fucked, and not even in the way I'd like to be. *What choice did I have now?* I didn't have a place to live, a job or any money.

For now. This was a temporary situation. I could handle him—for now. Keep him at bay—for now. At least knowing I was on shifting ground would make it easier to prepare for what happened once everything fell out from under me. Maybe I'd be able to grab onto the ledge when the time came, and save myself. I cleared my throat. Better get down to business if I was walking into this ring of fire.

"How much does this job pay?" I plopped down in my seat, resting my elbows on my knees. I took a sip of my wine to draw his attention away from my shaky hands. Rhys stared at me for a few seconds, an assessing look that made my stomach clench. He grabbed a piece of paper and pen from the coffee table, his hand flying across the notepad.

He got up and stood in front of me, my eyes level with his shining belt buckle. He held out the piece of paper between two of his fingers. He flicked them up and down, waiting for me to take the paper, and I imagined those two fingers inside of me doing the same exact thing. My pussy throbbed as I glanced up at him and took the paper from his hand, careful not to touch hm. I unfolded it and choked on the sip of wine I had in my mouth. The wine burned on its way down the wrong pipe as I hacked and coughed. Rhys took the glass of wine from my hand and gently patted me on the back.

"Per month," I wheezed, as he thumped my back.

"Per week," he said, chuckling. I'm sure I looked like I was having a fit. He handed my glass back and I chugged the contents. This could change my life. Even if I only stayed for a few months, I could finally catch the break I'd always needed to do things with my life. Maybe go to college, find a nice place to live. Living a life, instead of running from one. Forever caught in the trap I'd been stuck in since I was born.

"Okay. I'll take it," I said, my voice barely above a whisper, gazing up at him. He took a step closer, still towering over me, the hungry look back in his eyes, causing the wings of hundreds of butterflies to go crazy in my stomach. I licked my suddenly dry lips. He briefly closed his eyes, tipping his head back.

"Thank you, Melanie. You've made me very happy," he said, his hand coming up, meeting the side of my face. I hated how making him 'very happy' made me very tingly inside. I wanted him happy. I resisted the urge to nod my head like a good little girl. He'd come into my life, turning it upside down and disrupting the sliver of normalcy I'd created, but I wanted his approval. I felt it deep down, like his existence wasn't as perfect as I'd imagined. Every so often I caught a glimpse of him, the real him. His rawness didn't come from a life of perfection. He had cracks and he let me see every single one.

His hand hovered an inch from my skin and I ached to rest my cheek against his palm. To savor his hands on me, in a way beyond a polite interaction. Then he dropped his hand completely, holding it out for me to shake. I slid my hand into his and the second our skin touched I knew I was in trouble. Big trouble. Because the energy that pulsed between us wasn't something I could deny for long, and from the look in his eyes, I don't think he wanted to, either. It was a force that threatened to consume me.

I'd been through so much shit in my life, I was ready to finally make a choice about which ledge I leapt from. I'd been pushed off a cliff so many times before I even had my footing. This time I knew exactly where I stood—at least I hoped I did. I could already tell the fall from Rhys' cliff would hurt more than most. It would be from so much higher than I'd ever dreamed of diving, but I knew no matter what happened, my life would never be the same.

11

RHYS

I bit back a moan the second her pink tongue ran along her lips to wet them, giving them a glossy shine that drove me to the brink with a need to possess them. To possess her. As much as bringing her here had to do with Esme, the small voice in the back of my head told me it was also for me. All for me. She'd seen the burn in my eyes, the cracks in my mask, and she hadn't run.

Careful. Methodical. Precise. That had always been my way. As much as everyone thought I ruled my life with a golden touch, I didn't. I wrestled with that every day. Free falling and not being in control of my own destiny. But with Melanie, the free fall wasn't scary. It didn't push me toward despair. It was like the first gasp of air as you claw your way to the surface of the water. An injection of something I hadn't known I needed. To embrace the chaos. Being around her pushed me toward a side of myself I'd tried to shove deep down for so long.

I showed Melanie back to her room, shoving my hands in my pockets, so I didn't push her up against the wall, fist my hand in her hair until she cried out, and then delve deep into her mouth, breathing her in until I didn't know where she began and I ended.

As much as I wanted to bend her over the foot of her bed, I also had to think about the consequences. About how this could all blow up in my face, if I didn't ensure I put my daughter first. Melanie was under my roof and working for me now. The rest could wait. I was a patient man, I'd been instilled with self-denial since birth, I could wait a little longer. And then I'd have her. I'd make her mine.

Sitting behind my desk, scotch in one hand, tablet in the other, I flipped through yet another email. Another election. Another roadblock on my path to freedom. My pulse pounded as my anger coiled in my stomach, like a cobra ready to strike. My temples throbbed as I squeezed the tablet, the sound of cracking glass split the quiet of my wood-covered walls of my prison. I glanced down at the shattered screen. The board challenges were piling up and my suspicions of who was behind it all hadn't been confirmed yet, but I knew of only one person who'd dare run against me.

He lurked in the shadows, simmering anger at the public's opinion of me. Going to the same boarding school, we'd been close. Our merry band of troublemakers made my time there bearable, but things change. The summer his dad went to jail, all that changed, we changed, and here we were. One of my best friends growing up was now set on destroying me and everything I'd worked for. I sent a message to Rachel to get to work on digging deeper. I needed to know what he had planned.

Apparently, his being known in public as a complete

asshole didn't sit well with him, even though it was a fairly apt description. Whereas he was the asshole vilified in the press, I was the saint, but we both had the same dark soul. I was just much better at hiding it. Something made him decide to come after me now. I didn't know what it was, but it had to be something big for him to risk going up against me and destroying his reputation.

He didn't realize how much more was at stake for me than just my reputation. He thought I put on the mask to laugh at people behind their backs, but I put on the mask because it was the only way I knew how to survive. And I'd rain burning fire down on him to make sure I kept what was mine. Far from what people assumed, I'd had little of my own over the years. Even now, the life I created was a façade. Melanie was my chance for something, *someone* of my own.

She's yours, I repeated in my head. So close now. Only a few doors down. The way I grew up, I was on my own so much, left behind so many times. Since my wife died, another woman hadn't even slept in this apartment. Mel was different. She's a part of our family. I'd seen how she and Esme were together, so easy and happy. It had never been that way with my wife. By the time Esme was born, Beth was past the point of no return. Esme's time right after birth, in the neonatal intensive care unit for substances found in her blood, was smoothed over and kept out of the media and social services by a generous donation to the hospital. I hadn't been able to bring Beth back to reality no matter how much I tried. No matter how many barriers I'd put up to keep her safe.

She wanted out and she'd gotten out, but I hadn't been able to protect Esme like I should have. Derek and I tracking Beth and Esme down the night she ran away was the scariest of my life. Finding my little girl crouched over Beth's cold body in the rest stop bathroom ripped me in half. I'd failed.

I'd kept her overdose at the rest stop out of the news. I'd managed to keep that quiet, locked everything down under so much legal bullshit no one who knew would dare speak a word. I'd said it was an accident in our home. She fell in the bathroom and hit her head. A tragic end to the wife of a philanthropic billionaire. Nothing more, but I knew the truth and I'd do everything I could to protect Esme and her happiness. Happiness that meant keeping Melanie close. *Esme's happiness.*

It was because of the connection Melanie had with my daughter that I hadn't threaded my fingers through her hair when she sat in front of me, and claimed her mouth, nipping her as I breathed her in. My method of fuck her and forget her didn't seem like it would work this time. But I could be patient. I'd let her help us, and then I'd help myself to her.

But I had to be careful in my free fall. I couldn't scare her off, but I wanted her to know that this between us would happen. She felt it, too. I felt her pulse pounding when I shook her hand, and saw her shivers when she saw me watching her. She saw it, but soon she'd know it. Know what it felt like to belong to me. I hoped she could handle everything I was ready to give her, because I didn't think I'd be ready to let her go any time soon. I had no hope or intention of ever forgetting Melanie Bright.

12

MEL

I cracked my eyes open and saw the sun was barely above the horizon. No creepy stalker watching me, and that meant I could go right back to sleep. My nightmare was different this time. I could still smell the warm cinnamon rolls in the oven, but I hadn't woken in a cold sweat. Instead, I'd be able to roll back over in my warm new bed and go back to sleep.

I'd just closed my eyes again, when something huge landed on my side.

"Oof!" The air rushed out of my lungs.

"Good morning, Mel!" she said, so chipper, like she hadn't just tried to collapse one of my lungs. I flipped the blankets down to get a good look at her.

"Good morning, Esme." I glanced over at the clock on the nightstand. "Isn't it a little early?"

She was still in her heart-and-dragon pajamas, complete with a little robe and slippers. Her little arms wrapped around a white stuffed bear. My heart thudded as I looked at it. It wasn't the same one, I knew that was impossible, but it was so familiar it nearly brought tears to my eyes.

"No, not too early. My daddy said I'm not allowed out of my room until the little hand is on six, and it's past that already. What are we going to do today?" She vibrated with the energy only kids possess.

"I'm not sure yet. Maybe we should see if your dad has anything planned."

"Okay. Can I have some breakfast?"

"Sure, why don't we leave your stuffed animal in your room and I'll get you some food." I hated how much it got to me. How much it hurt to see that bear. I rolled out of the bed and Esme grabbed onto my hand.

We dropped off her bear and walked to the kitchen. The whole time she swung my arm back and forth, as she came up with all her plans for what she thought we should do today.

"Kiddo, we only have twenty-four hours in a day and it's almost winter. I don't think a day at the beach, plus the zoo, plus going to the library and stopping for ice cream are going to get done. Why not pick one of those and we'll put the rest on a list. What do you want to eat?" I stood in front of the wall of cabinets and a fridge that looked big enough to hold an entire side of beef.

"Can I have some pancakes?" Of course, she would start with the hard stuff. I opened a few cabinets, like a short stack would appear behind one of the doors.

"What about a cup of coffee or something?"

"I'm only little, Mel. I can't have coffee," Esme said, laughing like it was the funniest joke in the world. I pulled out my phone. Pancake recipe coming up.

"You have to help me, though. I can't do it all on my own." I grabbed the flour and other ingredients.

"Sure." Esme scooted a chair across the tile floor. I cringed, the sound of Esme's chair screeching across the floor loud enough to wake the dead. When Esme hopped up on the chair, I felt like I was like staring into a looking glass. It wasn't Esme there, it was me. So small and happy. I gulped past the tightness in my throat.

"I'll crack the eggs, but I'll need your help with the stirring." Esme nodded her head enthusiastically, sending her hair flying all over the place. "Should we add some chocolate chips?" She jumped up so fast she nearly fell off the chair. "I'll take that as a yes."

After the first ten pancake-flipping failures, I finally got the hang of the flipping. Esme gobbled them up almost as fast as I could make them, so I tried to keep them small. Bacon sizzled in the other pan I had going. I put some music on through my phone and did a little morning cooking dance, and Esme hummed as she shoveled the pancakes into her mouth. The snick of the syrup bottle being opened made me turn around. She drowned those semi-burnt oddly shaped pancakes.

"No more syrup. You're going to—" but it died in my throat. It wasn't Esme. It was Rhys. He stood beside her at the table. His hair a tousled mess, in pajama pants and no shirt, his tanned, muscled chest taunting me.

"Am I not allowed to have any?" he said, plate in hand.

"Of course, you can. I...I was just letting Esme know it wasn't a good idea to add another metric ton of syrup to her pancakes. They are already pretty sweet."

"They sure are." He cut off a small piece of the chocolate chip pancake and slid it into his mouth. My body heated up, like fire across my skin, and the spatula nearly fell out of my hand. "You're on fire, Melanie." She sure was, but how did he know that?

"What?"

He pointed his fork behind me. I turned to see a fiery

brick of charcoal in the middle of my pan, flames dancing around the edges of it. *Oh, shit!* I grabbed the pan off the burner and thrust it under the faucet turned on high. A cloud of steam and smoke blew up into my face. I washed the remnants of the pancake down the drain, dried off the pan, and went back to the burner, ladling some more batter and turned down the fire on the sizzling, popping bacon.

Rhys and Esme chattered about all her plans for the day. Esme popped up at lease twice more for-pancakes. I had no idea where she put the mountain of pancakes she devoured. Her body had to be about seventy-five percent pancake at this point. I just tried to focus on not burning the place down. I refused to turn around, keeping my focus solely on the pan and the pancakes. A chair scraped along the floor. I would have to cut her off. I didn't think it was right for a kid to eat twelve chocolate chip pancakes in one sitting.

"Can I take over?" It wasn't Esme, though. The hairs on the back of my neck stood up and I tightened my grip on the spatula. I glanced over my shoulder and my heart thundered. He nodded toward the pans and spatula.

"Sure, go right ahead," I said, handing Rhys the spatula before scooting my chair up to the table. His eyes were on me the entire way. I didn't have to look up to know. His gaze was hot and intense, and waited for Rhys to slide a pancake onto my plate. I thanked him, keeping my eyes firmly on my plate. Maybe I could drown out the feelings rushing through my body with a hearty helping of carbs and sugar. I stole a peek at him as I lifted the first bite to my lips. Mistake!

His muscled back, as he moved deftly from pan to pan, flipping pancakes and sliding the bacon onto a plate, drove me to distraction.

"Mel, can we go to the zoo? I decided."

"Sure, kiddo. We can go to the zoo."

"Daddy, are you going to come?"

I nearly choked on my food. I grabbed a glass of orange juice with both hands and gulped it down. I wasn't sure which was better, if he came or not.

RHYS

Waking up was always rough. Never being able to fall asleep unless I was at the point of exhaustion meant mornings were never my favorite. When I opened my eyes, the sun wasn't peeking over the horizon as it usually was when I first woke. It was in the sky. I checked my clock. After seven. Esme rarely let me sleep past the first crack of dawn.

I hopped up out of bed and raced to her room. My heart pounded in my chest. She wasn't there. The smell of bacon and sweetness snapped me out of it. Mel! How could I have forgotten?

Esme sat in her chair, wolfing down pancakes like they were going out of style, as music played from a phone on the table. Mel danced at the stove, her attention on the sizzling food in the pans. It hit me right in the chest, seeing the two of them there together. A deep ache for how things should have been. It all felt so normal. So right.

I kissed Esme on the top of her head as she shoveled pancakes into her mouth. Syrup stuck to the tip of her nose. Once Mel noticed I was there, she relinquished pancake duty to me.

I stood at the stove, spatula in hand. Esme and Mel sat at the table behind me, talking and having fun. I couldn't suppress my smile. It was so normal.

"Daddy, are you going to come?" Mel made a small choking at her question. So innocently asked, but Mel's reaction let me know exactly where her mind was. It was the same place my mind had gone when I walked into the kitchen and saw her in those pajama shorts and tank top, with her hair up on top of her head. *Beautiful.*

I wanted to go with them, but I couldn't. Duty called.

"I can't today, sweetheart, but I'm sure you'll have a great time with Mel."

The rest of breakfast went along quickly. Mel finished her plate of pancakes, not looking up at me once. Esme had her full attention. Every question, every comment, she was right there giving Esme her complete attention. It wasn't even something that I could do all the time. And Esme glowed under the attention. She was livelier than she'd been in quite some time.

Derek walked in like he did every morning ready for whatever the day had in store for us. Esme didn't talk, but she didn't close in on herself like she usually did.

"Derek, Melanie and Esme are going to head to the zoo today."

"I'll have the car ready as soon as you ladies are good to go," he said to Melanie.

"Great. Thanks. What do you say we go get ready, kiddo?" She wiped her mouth on a napkin and they cleaned up their dishes. "I can take care of this later."

"Don't worry about it. I'll take care of it."

And just like that, they were gone from the kitchen to go get ready.

"She looks pretty comfortable," Derek said, checking out

the table and the rest of the kitchen. It had a lived in feel it hadn't had before.

"It would seem so."

"Are you sure you want me to go with them? I can have five guys here in under an hour."

I didn't want anyone else watching over them but Derek. "I'm not going anywhere. I'll be in my office all day. At least with them, you'll get some fresh air." I'd be going through files. Making phone calls. Trying to make sure these challenges weren't going to screw up anything with my inheritance.

"If you say so," Derek grumbled as I walked back to my room. I passed by Esme's room and the sounds of laughter and talking were music to my ears. The apartment wasn't filled with silence anymore. Joy filled it to the point of overflowing.

I wanted more of that. I wanted more of that for Esme, and I wanted even just a sliver of it for myself.

13

MEL

The first days flew by. We settled into a routine that included, school, dinners and a lot of trips to the zoo. *A lot*. After another long day at the zoo and the bookstore, we made it back home. Esme's energy was boundless and I had to tag Derek in for a few minutes while I sorted through all our treasures from the day.

"May I please have some more tea?" Derek asked, squashed down on one of the tiny chairs at Esme's table. He had the patience of a saint.

"I like the ensemble, Derek. It suits you," I said, walking in with an armload of books. He shot me a glare. The kids apron with strawberries tight around his neck and a boa around his shoulder. We may have gone overboard at the store. But with Derek there to carry everything, we hadn't thought twice about piling our purchases high.

Bedtime was one of my favorite times with Esme. We'd gotten a bunch of books. Books my mom used to read to me every night when I was with her. She'd sit on the edge of my bed and read to me until I fell asleep. Being able to do that for Esme, made those memories easier.

The elevator dinged. Rhys was home. My stomach did the little flip it did whenever he was in the vicinity. I hadn't been here that long, but I didn't think I'd ever get used to it. I tucked the books away on the shelves.

"May I have some more tea?" Derek asked again, as he held out his tiny teacup. I couldn't hold back my laughter. Rhys's chuckle came from the doorway.

"Don't make fun." Esme frowned at both of us, got up from her chair and rounded the table to stand in front of Derek. She threw her arms around his neck and squeezed him in tight. The startled look on his face told me this hadn't happened before.

"I think you look really nice, Derek. Thank you for playing with me," she said, loud enough for me to hear. Loud enough for Rhys to hear. Derek froze and I heard Rhys suck in his breath. Derek sat there like he'd just been pulled out of a frozen lake. His body was rigid, until he wrapped his massive arms around Esme and hugged her back.

"Thank you, Esme." He gave her a squeezed as a watery sheen covered his eyes. He blinked hard before dropping his arms from around her back. She spoke in front of him. He'd been like our shadow since I got there. I figured Rhys wanted to make sure everything was on the up and up with me, but Derek had been a real friend since the first day.

"You're welcome, Derek," she said, beaming before sitting back down in her chair. They finished their tea party with Esme talking and Derek's voice tight, as though he spoke past a boulder lodged in his throat. Rhys stood there watching them while I tried to make myself busy getting things organized.

"Melanie, could I have a word?" Rhys asked, motioning for me from the doorway. I glanced over at Esme and Derek. She had added a pink boa to the other three that were already stretched across his broad shoulders. I wiped my clammy hands on my legs.

"Sure." I followed him out into the hall, nervous energy bouncing off me.

"Thank you," he said, like a breath he'd been holding for a long time.

"I didn't do anything." I hadn't really. I played with her. Walked her to school sometimes. Helped her with her homework, which she was completely able to do on her own.

"Whatever it is, keep doing it," he said, his eyes focused on Esme and Derek in her room. "How are you adjusting?"

"It's going well. We're still finding our routine." The babbling poured out of my mouth and I couldn't even stop it. The tingling in my fingertips made me want to reach out and smooth his furrowed brow. Something was wrong, but I didn't know what it was and I didn't know if it was my place to ask. I hesitated.

"Is everything, okay?"

My eyes met his and I nearly staggered back under the weight of what I saw there. I reached out a hesitant hand and put it on his shoulder. What the hell happened to make him so upset?

∼

RHYS

She spoke to Derek. Her high and light little voice rang out in the room as she wrapped her arms around Derek's neck. He got choked up. The impact of her words hit me right in my gut. He felt it, too.

Melanie had been here less than a month, and the

Esme's transformation was nothing short of a miracle. I couldn't thank her enough. I also couldn't let my desires when it came to her push aside how good she was for my daughter. My needs warred in my head.

Standing so close to her out in the hallway hadn't been a good idea. I should have never called her out there. She was so close and I wanted nothing more than to push her up against the nearest wall and show her how grateful I was for everything she'd done. I couldn't wait to tell her secrets I'd never told anyone, because maybe she could help fix me like she'd fixed Esme.

A wave of sadness rolled over me that Esme needed fixing in the first place. I wanted to pull Mel tight as the warmth of her hand sunk into my shoulder. Against my better judgment, I reached up and put my hand over hers. I ran my thumb across the back of her hand. I closed my eyes. I needed to stop this. I dropped my hand.

"Sorry. Yes, I'm fine." I cleared my throat.

"Are you joining us for dinner? We're making pizzas," she said, her eyes hopeful.

"I don't think so, but I'll try. I need to talk to Derek."

"Hey, Es. I know you're having fun with your party, but can I steal Derek away?"

"Okay. Mel, can you come play? Derek, will you come back?"

"We're making pizzas, remember?" Mel asked, walking into the room. "And we'll see Derek tomorrow. He's going to walk you to school, remember?"

"Yay, pizza!" Esme jumped up and raced to the kitchen. Everything beyond pizza forgotten.

I closed my office door after Derek, who brushed the multi-colored feathers off of his shoulders.

"She spoke to me." The awe in his voice brought tears to my eyes. She had. She'd spoken to him. *Mel did that!*

"I told you she liked you, Derek. There's nothing to worry about." I slapped him on the shoulder.

"You need to be careful, Rhys." Derek's voice held more concern than it usually did. "Mel..."

"I know." I squeezed the bridge of my nose. The intense pressure in my head battled against the lightness in my chest. "I don't know what to do about her."

"I'd start with not running her off like you usually do." Derek sat in the chair in front of my desk.

"I have no plans to do that with her. I'm not stupid."

"Then, I'd say you need to be careful. Really careful."

"I know." I leaned back in my chair. The cool leather warmed under my touch. *I'm sure Mel would warm under my touch too.*

"Stop it," he warned, shooting me a look. "I can tell exactly what you're thinking."

"I'm stopping. Melanie Bright is a woman just like any other, and I will not go near her in any manner other than a professional one." I pledged with my hand held up. Derek quirked his eyebrow up at me.

"I will. I can control myself." He didn't seem convinced. It was a double-edged sword. The more she did for Esme, the more I wanted to be near her. The more I wanted her in my arms. But it was more of a reason for me to stay away, to keep my distance. Today was just another one of Mel's miracles. I couldn't hold back my chuckle, remembering Esme sitting there with Derek folded into that tiny table.

"You looked good in there with that tiara."

"If that's what it takes, I'll do that and more for her,

man." And he was dead serious, even through the smile on his face.

"I know the feeling." I'd do whatever it took, including staying away from Mel. My hands itched to touch her skin. To touch and taste her, but I'd have to resist. I couldn't risk things going wrong and Esme losing her. And I'd put Esme first. I always did. *Stay away. It's that easy, isn't it?*

14

MEL

"Let's go to the park, kiddo. You've been cooped up in here all day," I said, dropping my magazine on my lap and nudging Esme with my foot. We'd been lying on her bed reading, for nearly the entire day. Well, she read. I dodged calls from Colleen. Her threats to come out to the city made me antsy. I needed to get out of here and away from my phone.

She'd drained my account, which meant she had money. I figured she wouldn't be able to find me, but I knew Jeanine and everyone else at the diner had seen my interacting with Rhys and Esme. Rhys hadn't exactly been subtle in quitting my job for me, and Martin was a blabbermouth. Everyone there knew where I was now. All she'd have to do is ask and they'd lead her right to me. It made me nauseous. I didn't want to see her. Ever. I'd moved to keep her states away from me. I didn't need her showing up and complicating my life even more.

"I don't want to go out. I want to stay here and read," Esme whined. "It's too cold outside and it's all snowy." We'd sat up watching the snow fall last night, sharing a bowl of popcorn between us. It was less than a month after Halloween, so I wasn't going to let it go to waste. *How often did I get to play in the snow?* Usually I dreaded it because it meant trudging to work in the slush and muck. Growing up, snow meant having to walk to school with my feet wrapped in plastic bags because of the holes in my shoes. But one of my favorite memories was of lying in the snow making snow angels and having a snowball fight with my mom. My real mom.

"Exactly. Let's go," I said, trying to get her up. She hadn't wanted to go trick-or-treating and I got the idea Rhys didn't like to push her too much. She ruled the roost, but she needed to get out. Get some fresh air, and be around other people, not just her dad, Derek and me.

"I don't want to," she said, going back to her book.

"That's okay. I definitely would have beat you in a snowball fight anyway. It wouldn't have even been a challenge. You're right to stay inside. I know you don't like to lose." I went back to my magazine, Esme quickly sat up and dropped her book.

"I would *not* lose," she said, her little cheeks turning a cute shade of pink.

"It's fine, Esme. It's okay. It's better this way," I said, watching her fall into my trap.

"Let's go. I'll show you. I'll kick your butt, Mel," she said in her sassiest voice, standing up and planting her hands on her hips.

"I mean, I guess if you *insist*, we can go. But no whining when you lose." She stomped out of the room, missing the laugh I'd been stifling since she'd put her book down. *Who knew that stuff worked on kids?* Maybe I *could* handle this nanny business.

The trip down to the park was a lot more trouble than I

expected. Calls had to be put in to Rhys and Derek. Getting Esme into her snowsuit might as well have been a journey into a sewage factory for how much she moaned about it, but we finally ventured out into the freezing, crisp fall air. The snowfall happened throughout the morning, so it was still pristine, not the brown mush it would turn into in a day or so.

We made it to the park with Derek trailing us. There were other kids in the park playing in the snow. A few snowmen were already there.

"Can we make a snowman?" Esme asked, tugging on my coat. I flexed my fingers in my thin, shitty gloves. They probably weren't the best for snowball fighting, but I was committed now. I dragged my hat down lower on my head to cover my ears and blew into my hands, attempting to warm them for a second.

"Trying to get out of our fight?" I asked, quirking my eyebrow at Esme. She was dressed like she was ready for an expedition to Antarctica. I was seriously jealous of the layers she had on. My clothes would have to do. I hadn't gotten paid yet, so I hadn't been able to go and pick up any winter-appropriate clothes as of yet. The new coat was a thoughtful gift, but it didn't come with new gloves or a hat, and I was too embarrassed to ask for an advance. I could tough it out.

The wet snow was already seeping into my shoes, chilling me as I wrapped my coat tighter around myself. I didn't think Esme would last too long, so I figured it wouldn't be too bad thawing out.

"Never," she challenged. It was good to see her with her game face on. I had to admit, Rhys had been right. Esme came out of her shell a little more every day I was there. It hadn't been long yet, but she was already talking more, sticking up for herself, and trying on her bossy pants. I loved that I'd been able to help. I still didn't know what I'd done, but I'd keep doing it until she didn't need me anymore.

Her father was a whole other story. I still didn't know what was going on with him. He was at the apartment most days. He loved spending time with Esme, whether they spent their evenings reading together or watching a movie. He always made time for her. They'd walk to school together, sometimes with me and sometimes on their own.

Every time Rhys looked at me, I fell down a rabbit hole of confusion and desire. One minute he looked at me like he wanted to eat me whole, and the next, it was like he hated me for it. I didn't understand, but thoughts of him clouded my brain. It was like he'd woven a spell over me. I tried to push him out of my mind whenever I could, but the entire apartment smelled like him. Minty, clean, fresh, those were all smells I associated with Rhys.

"This looks like a good spot," I said, finding a space with two rocks that would give us each shelter for our fight. "Let's get to work making some snowballs," I said, crouching down, the fresh snow crunching under my feet. I loved the way snow made everything look like a clean slate. Fresh and new even though underneath you knew it was the same old garbage.

We worked together making our arsenal of snowballs. Derek even chipped in, packing them methodically and adding all of them to Esme's pile. Kids ran by with sleds and inflatables, headed to the small hill nearby. All in all, it was a picture-perfect afternoon. The sun shined high in the sky, giving off a little warmth, but my ears were freezing, my nose had to be the brightest shade of red, and my hands were numb. A few other kids had joined us, excited for a snowball fight. By the time we had our ammo ready, I could barely flex my fingers.

"Why did you come out here with gloves like those?" Derek asked, finishing up the last snowball. I shrugged. It wasn't like I had much of a choice. I glanced down at his gloveless hands and raised my eyebrow at him. He flexed his fingers with ease and they didn't look the least bit red like mine. *Was he a cyborg?* I wouldn't put it past Rhys to have the first cyborg bodyguard.

"I didn't really have time to go clothes shopping yet. I didn't have time for snowball fights before. I wasn't prepared."

"Let me see your hands," he said. I held them out, taking my gloves off so he could inspect them. Derek cursed under his breath. "Are you trying to get frostbite? Thayer will kill me if anything happens to you," he grumbled under his breath, shaking his head.

"What?"

"Nothing. I'm going to get you some real gloves, not these bullshit fake leather things. I'll be right back. Don't you two move, okay?"

"We won't move, scouts honor," I said, holding up my two fingers. "We'll start our fight without you, though," I teased.

"Fine, just don't leave this area," he said, glancing around, before jogging off. Derek was a good guy. Annoying at times, but I knew why he was the way he was. I'm sure being security for someone like Rhys wasn't easy. The threats against a billionaire must be unpredictable, to say the least. I wasn't going to bust his balls, or make his job harder for him.

"Ready, kiddo?" I asked Esme, crouching down behind my rock.

"Ready!" Esme exclaimed, scrambling behind hers with the other kids.

"You guys ready?" I said to the kids and some parents who'd joined us.

"Snowball fight commencing in three-two-one. Go!" I shouted and there was a hail of snowballs whizzing by. Snow flying everywhere, a cold spray of it hit my face as snowballs exploded around me. Esme's bright pink hat popped up from behind the rock every few throws. She even managed to get a direct hit right in my face. *Good arm, kid.* Laughter rang out from every corner of the park, kids face planted and there was complete chaos until the snowball supply dwindled down to nothing.

"Esme, do you surrender?" I shouted from behind my rock, one final snowball clutched in my hand. There was no response, only the laughter of the other kids. *She's already leaving me behind to hang with her friends.* "Esme, do you surrender?" I repeated, rounding her rock, but she wasn't there. My stomach plummeted and every sound around me washed away as the blood pounded in my ears. I whipped my head around, calling her name. Then, before I even realized it, I was screaming her name. My voice cracked as I yelled out for her, spinning in circles, my hands on my head trying to think clearly. *Where was she? Why would she leave? What if something had happened to her? Please let her be okay. Please.*

Other parents started to glance around too. The parents and kids from our game called her name. Her pink hat sat on the ground, only feet away from where we'd made our snowballs. I snatched it up off the ground, clutching it to my chest. *Oh God, where was she?* The overwhelming urge to vomit climbed up my throat. I screamed her name again.

I ran toward the people sledding, and out of the corner of my eye, I saw her. She was still here. She stood under a tree. Relief washed over me, but dread replaced it as I saw the man crouched in front of her. I'd been so focused on her, my mind hadn't even registered that there was someone else with her at first. He stood and his hand held onto her jacket, tugging her away. Away from me.

I took off running, my hair whipping around my face as my hat fell to the ground. I stepped on it, not caring for one second. Everything moved in slow motion as my feet connected with the ground, sliding in the snow. *Please be okay. Please be okay.* I prayed as my legs pumped harder than I'd ever run before in my life. My heart thundered in my chest as I got closer to them.

The man had a hold of Esme's coat, and she tried to pull herself away from him. I launched myself at him, ripping his hand off her coat and knocking him to the ground. My breath came out in heavy pants, a cloud of my breath forming in front of my face with each word.

"Get the fuck away from her," I screeched. I grabbed Esme and stood in front of her, ready to rip this guy's balls off. "Don't you dare touch her. Who are you? What were you doing with her?"

"I wasn't taking her anywhere. I was just trying to talk to her," the guy said, getting up off the ground, brushing the snow off his black puffy coat. He had on a black hat and tan boots. I whipped my phone out of my pocket to take a picture. My hands shook so hard that it fell into the snow. I tried to commit every bit of detail about him to memory to relay to Derek and the cops. This stuff came up on the news from time to time, but I'd never thought something like this would happen here. Esme's hands gripped my coat, her tiny fingers trembling. I couldn't tell if it was from the cold or from fear. I hoped it was the cold. But knowing this guy terrified her made me want to rip his throat out.

"You don't talk to her. You don't know her. Don't ever talk

to her," I shouted. A flash of gray whizzed past me and Derek was there. I relaxed a bit, turning to hold Esme in my arms. Derek had his hands around the guy's collar. His feet left the ground as Derek slammed him up against the closest tree.

"Get her out of here," he growled at me. My breath came out in stuttering puffs as I allowed myself to breathe again. Derek would handle this. I turned and scooped Esme up in my arms, adrenaline helping me carry her all the way back to the apartment. I didn't stop until I got back inside, setting her down in the foyer. I tucked her hair back behind her ears, noticing the twin tracks of tears drying on her skin. It made me want to go back down there and help Derek with whatever he decided to do to the guy.

"Hey, Esme. You're okay now. You're safe," I said, getting down on my knees and hugging her to me, rocking her back and forth.

"What happened, kiddo?" I asked softly, leaning back to let her speak. But she clamped her lips shut. "It's okay, if you don't want to talk. How about I make you a bubble bath and some hot chocolate?" I offered, trying to catch her eyes. She looked up at me and nodded her head. I got her out of her snowsuit and ran her a bath. As I went to hang up her snow stuff, Derek burst into the apartment, making me jump.

"Is she okay?"

"She's in the bath. Who was that guy?"

"He was no one. Everything is fine now. He's been taken care of," Derek said, handing me back my phone. I didn't want to ask questions. Whatever happened to the guy, he had it coming. But something told me he wasn't no one.

"Do the police want to speak to Esme or me?" Derek shook his head. "No police. It's done." A shiver ran down my spine, but I wasn't going to argue. He left, but not before letting me know that security had been stepped up in the building, and not to leave the penthouse. He didn't have to tell me twice.

After Esme's warm bath, I tucked her into bed and went to make her hot chocolate. The elevator doors slid open and Rhys stormed into the foyer, his eyes laser focused on me. I stepped back, hitting my head against the kitchen cabinets. *Rage.* He seethed. Anger radiating off him, and it was all aimed straight at me. My stomach churned and I dropped my eyes. My hand wrapped around the mug holding Esme's hot chocolate, burning as drops of hot liquid splashed up and over the top. Rhys's heavy breathing cut through the subdued atmosphere of the apartment.

"Where is she?" he growled.

"In..In her room. I was making this for her," I said, holding out the mug, the pain in my hand long since forgotten. He rushed down the hall and into her room. I stood there frozen, I didn't know where to go. The look he'd given me, it was like he'd reached into my chest and squeezed my heart with his bare hands. I added a couple ice cubes to her mug and crept down the hall, stopping in the doorway. Rhys had Esme in his arms, cradling her, rocking her back and forth, and speaking in hushed tones. She saw me standing there and held out her hand to me.

"Thank you, Mel," she said, taking a sip of the hot chocolate. The knot that formed in my stomach loosened an inch as her words rolled over me. It was a temporary setback. What happened today hadn't knocked down the progress we'd made so far. I sat in silence, perched on the end of her bed as Esme finished her hot chocolate and recounted our snowball adventure in the park to Rhys. Like the other part of the day hadn't happened. Like it was forgotten. I hoped it was. I hoped it wouldn't give her nightmares like the ones that plagued me. Rhys was all smiles for her, but every glance at me turned my stomach. Esme yawned and snuggled down in bed.

We tucked her in and walked out into the hall. The second Rhys closed her bedroom door, he was on me. He grabbed my arm in a punishing grip and stalked down the hall with me, flinging me into his office.

"Did you tell him to meet you there? What was your plan?" he roared, slamming his fist into the wall. I jumped, my heart thundering in my chest. I had never seen this side of him before. I'd never been afraid of him before, not like this. He thought I had something to do with the guy in the park today. He thought I'd tried to have her kidnapped.

"I didn't have anything to do with what happened today. I...I was just trying to help Esme have some fun. I didn't know something like this would happen! She was out of my sight for a few minutes in a park filled with people. I'd have never thought someone would try to take her. If I had, of course I never would have gone," I said, my voice quivering.

"Why did you send Derek away?" he asked, his arms crossed over his chest, scrutinizing me, dissecting me. It turned my stomach. This wasn't like before. He'd never looked at me like that before.

Tears welled in my eyes. I knew it was too good to be true. Someone like him wasn't going to trust someone like me. I'm surprised I'd lasted this long. He backed away from me, fire still raging in his stare, and I lowered my arms. I willed the tears back in my eyes, closing them in a long blink.

15

RHYS

It took everything in me not to punch a hole through the wall. He'd approached Esme. Talked to her. Probably scared her half to death. I had never seen him in person. But the pictures of him and my dearly departed wife, kissing and rolling around in bed together, were seared into my brain. As much as his fucking face had been burned into my memory, I still was not prepared for him to show up out of the blue. And I damn sure wasn't prepared for him to be anywhere near Esme.

Derek took a picture of the guy. His bloody nose and bleeding cut on his forehead weren't enough to make him unrecognizable, I knew it was him, the man who'd taken so much from me and could take so much more.

Mel stared back at me, her eyes wide and her lips trembling. *Was she a lot more devious than I thought?* How did she know Allan? What was her connection to him and how long had she been planning this? From the start? I didn't know, but I needed to find out. His presence upended the thin thread of control I had over anything happening in my life right now.

"Answer me," I shouted and she jumped. I hated that I made her feel this way, but I needed to be sure. I needed to know she wasn't a threat. As much as I wanted her, I'd never put her ahead of Esme. I'd die before I let anything happen to my little girl.

"I didn't. I didn't," she said, taking a big gulp of air. "My hands were cold. Derek was being nice and offered to get me gloves. That's all." I was usually a good judge of character. I'd had to be over the years, especially with what happened with Beth.

I also learned that people loved to fill in a silence. They couldn't stand to have it fill the air. I observed her. Tried to ferret out any deception on her part because that would be all I needed to have her put in a hole so deep, she'd dream of seeing sunlight again. But nothing about her screamed that she'd been involved. Derek told me the scene he came upon when he got back to the park. How she had Esme behind her, protecting her. I wanted that to be true. I wanted that to be the whole story. But I'd been burned before. *Was my infatuation clouding my judgement?*

"Who was he?" I asked, trying again, attempting to calm my voice.

"I don't know what you're talking about. I don't know who that was. I'd never seen him before in my life. I didn't have anything to do with what happened this afternoon. I was so scared. The most scared I've ever been in my life," she said, emphatically.

I stared at her, soaking her in. I don't know how long it was, but she held my gaze. Unwavering. I saw the shine of tears in her eyes. It wasn't guilt I saw there but fear, fear for Esme and what happened today. I ran my hands through my hair. I had to believe she hadn't done this. I couldn't stand it if she were involved.

Taking her out of the equation still left me with Allan. From the talk he had with Derek, he was clean now. *Congratu-fucking-lations, Allan.* It would have been nice if he'd been clean when he started his affair with my late wife. Beth's childhood sweetheart. Had I known what would happen, how she'd rip my life apart, I'd have never married her, but then I wouldn't have Esme. Every shitty thing that happened in my life up until the moment Esme was laid in my arms wasn't something I could entirely regret.

Allan was a problem, though. I'd thought was dead by now. An overdose or something else, but he was here now. He knew all my wife's secrets, ones I thought died with her, and ones that could destroy everything. Derek scared him off for now, but he'd be back. I had no doubt in my mind, he'd be back. I didn't know what to do and that uncertainty shook me to my core.

"Okay, I believe you. I'm sorry," I said, squeezing the back of my neck. My muscles bunched so tight, I felt like I'd snap something at any moment. She staggered back against the wall. And the tears that had welled up in her eyes finally spilled over. Her shoulders shook as she clasped her hands over her mouth. I shouldn't have. I shouldn't have gone near her, but I couldn't help it. I'd contributed to her sorrow. I was part of the reason she broke down like this.

I wrapped my arms around her, holding her tight against me as she cried into my shoulder. She gripped the back of my shirt, fisting it in her hands. Her tears soaked through my shirt and onto my chest. The wetness tickled my skin.

I could kick myself for losing my temper and scaring her. I let the fear of Esme being harmed or worse, taken, over power my emotions to the point that I couldn't think or see straight. I lost my shit, and being the asshole that I am, I took it out on Mel.

That being said, I didn't think her breakdown was entirely because of me.

I understood the heart-pounding, and panic that weave themselves together into a blanket that threatens to choke you when your child disappears. I felt the same way I had that moment when Derek told me Esme was gone. The day I met Mel.

After a few minutes, Mel's shoulders stopped shaking and she wiped her face with her hands. I grabbed a few tissues for her and she mumbled a 'thanks' before letting out the almightiest of nose blows that left my ears ringing.

I cracked a smile and went over to my bar and grabbed two glasses. I uncorked the crystal decanter and poured a finger of whiskey for us both. Melanie finished wiping the tears from her face and glanced up as I dangled the tumbler in front of her. She took it from me using both hands and downed it in one gulp, coughing and thumping her chest. I threw mine back and enjoyed the slow burn that spread through my chest, spreading out to my fingers.

"Thanks," she said, giving me a small smile. I nodded and took the glass from her. I hated the way she was looking at me, that I could still see the lingering signs of fear and hurt in her eyes. I hated that she saw that side of me. That I can't be that knight in shining armor the rest of the world sees me as. But the way she looks at me, tells me she sees the real me.

"I figured it was the least I could do," I said. If she didn't quit after this, I'd be really fucking lucky. I accuse her of trying to kidnap Esme and she has a breakdown in my arms. "Thanks for looking after her today, Mel. I don't know what I'd do if something happened to her," I said.

Her head whipped up and she gawked at me. I glanced behind me trying to figure out why she looked at me like I had two heads. "What?"

"That's the first time you've ever called me Mel," she said, a small smile playing on her lips.

"Is it?" I didn't feel like that was true. I always called her Mel in my head when I thought about her. I moaned *Mel* when my restraint was at its breaking point and I had to take myself in my hand and dream about being with her, about touching her soft curves, as I stroked myself, lost in the vision of her. Her name had been on my lips more times than I wanted to think about. She invaded my thoughts to the point that I wondered if I would ever be able to think about anyone else.

16

MEL

His apology and peace offering cleared the air between us. I didn't know what it was like, entrusting your kid to someone else's care, but I imagined it came with a whole lot of worry about whether they were good enough, responsible enough, honest enough.

"I hadn't realized," he said, gesturing to one of the chairs. The cool leather squeaking as I slid into the seat.

"She had a lot of fun at the snowball fight. It was nice to see her playing with other kids."

"She doesn't do that very often. Thanks for getting her out. She loves to stay cooped up in the house and I don't push her to do more," he said, squeezing the bridge of his nose.

"I can't imagine what it's like for you. You're doing the best you can," I said, cringing. Of course, he was. He had more money than God. Esme had the best of everything and above all else, she had a daddy who she knew without question loved her. He didn't need my seal of approval. "How are you doing?"

"I'm fine. Now that I know Esme's safe. That you're safe. I'm sorry if I scared you before."

"It's okay. I don't know what I'd do if something happened to my own kid." Was this what my mom felt that day at the grocery store? That clawing panic that threatened to bring you to your knees?

"The fact that it's happened twice in the past couple of months has put me on edge." The ice rattled in his glass as he gazed out the window. "I must be the world's worst father." He drowned the pain in his voice with another sip.

"Don't think that. Don't ever think that. You have no idea how terrible some parents can be. None. Esme is healthy, happy, warm, safe and loved. That's more than a lot of kids could ever hope for." I said it emphatically, probably more than I needed to.

"I'll get you another drink," he said, again not asking. I was beginning to get used to his controlling nature. Sometimes he just seemed to know what I needed, even before I realized it.

When Rhys stood in front of me to take my glass, our fingers touched as he took it from my outstretched hand. Once again, I froze, staring into his eyes, as he towered over me. He put both our glasses down on the table behind him and ran his hand along my jaw.

"I don't know what we'd do without you, Mel." His touch sent a tingling down my spine as he said my name again. The way it rolled off his tongue. I licked my lips and his thumb ran along my chin, just under my bottom lip. I don't know if it was instinctual or if I just really wanted to do it, but I couldn't help it. I dipped my tongue out and ran it over my lips. The fire was back in his eyes now, the fire that made my stomach somersault and my core throb.

He sucked in a breath and ran his thumb over my wet

lip. A hint of his flavor danced on my lips and I couldn't hold back anymore. Maybe it was the highly charged emotional day I had, or maybe it was the fact that I'd wanted him since the moment I saw him, but never thought it possible. I wanted comfort. I wanted his comfort, in whatever way I could get it. I stuck my tongue out and licked his thumb, drawing it into my mouth and sucking on it. A mix of scotch and Rhys hit my tongue. I longed to taste even more of him as he groaned. I loved that I could draw that out of him, make him putty in my hands. Wielding a power I didn't even know I had.

Rhys pushed his thumb into my mouth deeper and I sucked on it harder, keeping my eyes on him, not wanting to break the trance we were both under.

"You're playing with fire, Mel," he warned. When he said my name like that I couldn't help but turn liquid under his gaze. I let his thumb fall from my mouth.

"I know, but I can take the heat," I said, resting my hands on his belt buckle. I was out of my mind, but I was past the point of caring. I needed this, and I think he needed this too. One second I was looking up at him, and the next, my back was pressed against the top of his desk, my legs wrapped around him and his heavy weight settled on top of me. I savored his body on top of mine.

He kissed his way along my neck. His lips like liquid fire, threatening to consume me. I tilted my head to give him better access. He nipped my neck and I ran my fingers through his hair, pulling him in closer to me. Everything was Rhys. Every smell, every taste and everything completely focused on him and what he was doing to my body. I thrummed with a pounding energy that couldn't wait to be set free.

A loud knock on the door broke us apart. I was still in a

daze on top of his desk before I realized he was gone. The cool air of the room hit me, and embarrassment settled in. *Did I really just do that? Suck on his thumb like that? What was I thinking?* He glanced back at me before opening the door. Derek stood there with a file folder and I knew our time was over. I hustled out of the room with my cheeks on fire.

It was hours before I fell asleep. Staring up at the ceiling, wondering what would happen now. Now that I'd thrown myself at my new employer like that, and now that he'd been more than happy to take me up on my offer. My stomach was still aflutter from what happened in the office. He wanted me just as much as I wanted him. *What surprises would tomorrow bring?*

~

RHYS

Derek kept his face a mask of professionalism as Mel raced out of the office like her hair was on fire.

"What?" I said, snatching the file out of his hand. Everything I'd tried to do to prepare myself with her being so close was thrown out the window. I wanted her. I wanted her more than I'd wanted anything in a long time. All the things I'd told myself about her and how I needed to stay away blared even louder in my head and I didn't know how much longer I could resist.

"I didn't say anything," he said, shrugging. He folded his arms across his chest, standing like a sentry. I flipped open the folder.

"What's all this?" I asked, turning each page, not making sense of anything in there.

"This is what Allan's been up to for the past few years. I had the file put together, so you'd know what was going on."

"How did he find her, Derek?" That worried me more than anything. He'd known where to find Esme, and approached her. Scared her and Mel half to death. Scared all of us. *What was he trying to do?*

"You're not exactly low-profile. Where you live isn't a secret."

"What a clusterfuck. What did you say to him?" I closed the folder. Nothing in there told me anything I needed to know. *What had he said to Esme? Had he said anything to Mel?*

"I wasn't exactly having a conversation." He tugged at his sleeve. "He scared Esme, and Mel freaked out. I wasn't just going to pat him on the head and let him go on his way."

"Did the cops get involved?" That would be a media circus.

"No, I smoothed that over."

"Good," I said, the tightness in my chest relaxing the smallest bit.

"The costs were high, though," he said, glancing up at me. The worry in his eyes was plain as day.

"How much?" He told me the amount and I started running calculations in my head. Looked like I would be doing a lot of donating over the next few weeks. *A lot.*

"We'll keep them safe, don't worry about that. I'll work off the clock if I need to." The glint in Derek's eye told me he meant every word of it. He'd become so much more than a security guard. He was a friend. Probably my only friend at this point.

"I appreciate it, Derek. But I'll make it work."

I only hoped that Allan popping up didn't mean he intended to be around. I hoped he was passing through or this was a momentary lapse in judgement. If he intended to stick around, I was prepared to reign down everything in my arsenal to ensure he didn't do any more harm to my family than he'd already done.

And I needed to keep away from Mel. I saw how she helped Esme after what happened. She got her talking again in a matter of hours. I couldn't risk screwing this up and having her leave. Esme needed her and I needed her here. If I had to keep my distance, then that's what it meant because I wasn't going to drive away the one person who'd given my daughter back to me.

17

MEL

I couldn't sleep. The nightmares were back. Funny, most people's nightmares were of scary things. Things they feared and couldn't forget. My nightmares were worse than that. They were things I wanted to forget because they were too painful to remember. Too bright and sunny. Too happy. Being tucked in at night. Baking cookies. Running home from school because I was so excited to do my homework and have dinner at the table. One year of perfection in an otherwise bleak sea of desperation and pain.

I flung the covers off me and slid out of bed. I needed to get a drink. It became something of a nightly tradition for me. I'd slip out of my room, check on Esme and grab a drink from the bar. A little liquid courage to help me face those dreams again. Rhys had been gone a few days, so I wasn't afraid to wander.

I walked past the gym and a light was on. Esme left that thing on more than she turned it off. The trampoline was one of her favorite energy burners since the snow and ice settled over the city. Yes, an indoor trampoline. My fingers had just grazed the light switch when I froze in front of the large window overlooking the lap pool. Thick legs sliced through the water, efficient and powerful. He was back.

I stood there, mesmerized as he swam lap after lap. Sinewy muscle glided across the pool, his long arms slicing through the water. He was a machine. I don't know how long I watched him. But it was so long, I anticipated his next turn in the water and was caught off guard when he pulled himself out of the pool. Droplets sliding down his back. My eyes followed the path of the water as it ran down over his ass. My cheeks flamed as it dawned on me that he wasn't wearing any trunks.

The water cascaded over his firm ass as he turned and sat on the edge of the pool and grabbed for a towel. He picked it up and dried his face, then looked up and stared directly at me. He knew I was there. I fled from the gym, my nightmares forgotten and replaced with dreams of muscled arms and his strong frame settled on top of me, giving me exactly what I needed.

He didn't mention the night at the pool the next time I saw him. And I certainly wasn't going to. But the tension between us remained. That night in the office, coupled with our encounter at the pool. Every time I saw him I couldn't get the visions of him out of my head, the way his lips felt against my neck, the way he tasted. He seemed immune though. Like he was often seen in his full glory by women who worked for him. He'd been the picture of professionalism. If I hadn't known better I'd have thought everything that passed between us, all our inappropriate moments were all in my head.

~

Decorations and Christmas trees popped up all over the city. The messages on my phone were more frequent and urgent. Since I opened a new bank account, the old one stayed drained. I wasn't making that mistake again. If there was one thing I thanked Colleen for it was finally curing me of the last vestige of a connection between us. For some reason, I had thought if I worked hard enough maybe she could be like a decent human being, but that idea was dismissed a long time ago.

Colleen: I saw you in a picture with that rich guy. Finally made it back to where you always thought you belonged, didn't you?

Me: Leave me alone, Colleen.

Colleen: Maybe I should come over there and tell him all about you.

Me: Don't contact me again.

Colleen: Don't tell me what to do. You always thought you were better than me. I'll be seeing you soon. You'll be kicked to the curb just like you always are.

And with that nasty reply, I turned off my phone. *Thanks, Mom.* I hadn't thought of her as my mom in a long time. Not after the first time I was taken away from her and put into foster care. Back then I didn't know it wasn't normal for a seven-year-old to have to make her own food scrounged out of whatever was in the house at the time. That taking a bath once a week wasn't how it was supposed to be. But she still tried to find a way to screw up my life, even from halfway across the country. The threat of showing up had me transferring a little bit of money into the joint account. It was the only way I knew to get her to leave me alone. The last thing I needed was her showing up in the city trying to track me down. All I needed was a few months to get things together, and I could tell her exactly where to go. Forever.

"Mel, can we go ice skating today?" Esme asked, bounding into the room. It was hard for me to believe this little girl hadn't talked to anyone but me or her dad in over two years. When she was with me, she was just a normal little kid. Bouncy, manic, and adorable all rolled into one.

"Sure, I need to check with your dad first. I think he had some plans for the two of you later today."

"Ugh," she said, flinging herself on my bed, ever the actress. Esme ran back to her bedroom and I made my way to Rhys's office. Since that night of the run in with the guy in the park, things between us had been more confusing than ever. The way he looked at me, spoke to me, and made me feel, my stomach was a mess whenever I was around him. Going in search of him was a dangerous prospect. The days after that night in the pool hadn't been as awkward as I imagined because he'd made himself scarce. He had a couple of days where he travelled and was otherwise locked up in his office.

But now I needed to speak to him. Rachel and Derek had been great go-betweens over the past few weeks, but I needed to speak to Rhys eventually. Why not now? The solid wooden door to his office loomed in front of me. And remembering what happened behind that door had those butterflies awakening. Stretching and gently flapping their wings. I didn't like to disturb him when he worked, which seemed to be non-stop. I hated to think it was always like this. I raised my hand to knock, when the light from inside caught my eye. It was cracked open.

"I don't give a fuck what they intend to do. I need to be on that board for next year. I told you to get results and so far, you've given me nothing. Get it done!" Heavy breathing and then an ear-splitting crash made me yelp before I could stifle the sound.

The door whipped open with a glowering Rhys standing there looking more feral than I'd ever seen him. His demeanor shifted immediately and while his eyes still burned, he didn't look like he was ready to tear me apart. Sparkling pieces of glass littered the floor behind him. He glanced over his shoulder and closed the door behind him, pushing out into the hall and right against me before I took a step back.

"Sorry, I didn't mean to interrupt. I— Esme wanted to go ice skating, but you mentioned a gala earlier and I didn't know what time you'd need her ready," I blurted out. He tilted his head to the side and crossed his arms over his chest.

"I never said anything about Esme going to the gala. I said I needed you to be ready at eight."

"But—" My brain tried to recall the conversation. I'd been so distracted by him I completely missed that part. *A gala. I couldn't go to a gala.*

"I can't go to a gala. I'm not really gala material. I don't have anything to wear."

"There's a dress hanging in your closet along with shoes. Rachel dropped them off yesterday," he strode past me and I scrambled to catch up. *Yesterday?* I hadn't seen anything in the room.

"Rhys, wait," I said, grabbing onto his arm. He stopped abruptly and I slammed into his back. He turned to steady me, his hands on my shoulders. Prickling fire crested over me at his fingers on me.

"You know that's only the second time you've ever said my name," he said. His smoldering gaze on me.

"It is?" I squeaked.

"Yes. You always call me 'your dad' whenever you speak to Esme or you don't call me anything at all. I liked hearing my name on your lips," he said, bringing his mouth closer to mine. My breath caught in my throat as I breathed in his intoxicating scent and watched his lips as he spoke. "I'd like to hear you say it again."

"Rhys," I whispered. His soft lips, turned up, a little higher to one side. Almost a smirk and it turned everything upside down. It wasn't a smile of happiness, at least not all happiness. It was a smile that promised me he had so many more plans for us. Beyond our toe-curling kiss and skinny dipping. I clasped my hands behind my back to keep from fanning myself.

"There will be someone here in thirty minutes to do your hair and makeup. Check your closet for the dress," he said, his breath fanning against my face. Goosebumps prickled my skin and his fingers rubbed against my shoulders. "I hope you like the dress."

And then he was gone, striding off down the hall to his own room. I took a few seconds to collect myself before finding Esme and letting her know we wouldn't be able to ice skate. But I promised we would go soon, and threw another trip to the zoo to sweeten the pot. I stood in front of my closet, equal parts excited and scared to open the door and see just what he'd picked out for me.

I laid the unassuming black garment bag on the bed and my fingers trembled as I unzipped it. The bright red peeked out from the zipper before I whipped the dress out and held it in front of me. The red lace gown had a high neck with see through lace covering the shoulders. It was gorgeous, not something I'd have picked for myself, but beautiful. I picked it up to hold it up in the mirror when I noticed the back of the dress was nowhere to be found. There was a plunging back that had me searching the bag to make sure something wasn't missing.

The knock on the door signaled the arrival of the team Rachel had called in.

"We've got a lot to do, Mel. I mean, not that you need a lot done. It's just I want to make sure tonight's perfect for you," Rachel said, flustered and turning a deep shade of pink, pushing her glasses up her nose. She had to be the most dedicated assistant in the business. Rhys ran her ragged at times, but she never complained. Not that she would, at least not to me.

"It's okay, Rachel. I knew what you meant. I'm glad you've done all this. I wouldn't have known the first thing about getting ready for something like this," I said, sitting in the hairstylist's chair that had appeared out of nowhere.

"Great! You're going to have so much fun tonight. Mr. Thayer—I mean Rhys wanted to make sure everything was perfect," she said, clapping her hands together, her phone between them.

"I'm sure you've got these guys on speed dial for these types of things," I said, as they wrapped the cape around my shoulders. She gave me a funny look. Did I have something in my teeth?

"No, never. Rhys has never done something like this for anyone before. He picked out the dress himself, told me to ensure you had everything a woman would need for a gala," she said, scrolling through her phone. Her phone buzzed, "Sorry, I've got to take this."

The next four hours were a whirlwind of activity. I was tweezed, waxed and pinched to within an inch of my life. Any protests were met with a quick rebuke from Rachel, who popped in and out on phone call after phone call, when she wasn't typing away on her phone. Her eyebrows got more and more furrowed throughout the afternoon as the sun set. The poor woman had enough to deal with when it came to Rhys. I didn't want to make things any more difficult.

Rachel walked in after what felt like days in the chair. She clutched her phone between her hands.

"Wow, you look amazing, Mel," she said, standing in front of me with a huge smile plastered on her face.

Whirling around in my chair, I came face to face with someone who looked like an oddly smooth and way fancier version of myself. I was tempted to run a hand over my face, but a quick smack to the back of my hand from the makeup artist stopped me. And an artist she was. It was hard to believe it was my own reflection in the mirror, staring back at me.

Without thinking I raised my hand again. The makeup artist tutted me before packing up and heading out. Then, it was time to put on the dress. After some maneuvering to keep my hair and makeup intact, Rachel zipped me up. I slid on my heels and wobbled a bit. I wasn't a heels kind of girl, but I figured tonight called for them. Rachel, taking mercy on me, slipped a pair of foldable flats into my clutch, along with another tube of lipstick and some blotting tissue. Seriously, that's all that fit into that thing. Rachel shoved it into my hand and hustled me out into the foyer. We passed by Esme's room on the way and she ran out, giving me a huge hug.

"You look like a princess, Mel! So pretty!" she said, beaming up at me. Esme's comment, along with the amount of pampering I had just received had truly made me feel like one, a real princess. The giant knot of nervousness eased up a tiny bit.

"Thanks, kiddo. I think it's your bedtime, isn't it?" I said, checking out the night sky through her window.

"Yeah," she said in a huff, stomping her foot on the floor.

"Don't worry, I bet Rachel is a great story reader, but you'll have to tell her how you like the voices to go, okay?"

"Okay," she sighed, glumly. "Have fun at the party with Daddy." She bounded back into her room, shuffling through her bookshelf, probably looking for the longest story she could get her hands on. We made it to the foyer, with Rachel fussing over me the whole way.

"Don't let her try to squeeze more than one book out of you. She'll try to milk it and get as many as she can, so she can stay up. She likes you to do deep voices for the bad guys and don't worry about sounding silly. She loves it when you ham it up," I said, worrying about leaving Esme alone tonight.

It would be my first night away since I'd started. Had someone told me a few months ago that I'd be worried about leaving her behind for a night without reading her a bedtime story, I'd have laughed. But here I was. Worried about a little girl who'd become such a huge part of my life over the past few months. She and her dad, the dynamic duo, were turning my life upside down.

"Working to keep Esme happy at all times aren't you, Mel?" Rhys's voice sent shivers down my spine, the rich thickness of it coating me in complete awareness of his presence.

"I try," I said, glancing over my shoulder, nearly choking as Rhys stepped out from the hall. "Black-tie" suited him. He wore his tuxedo like a second skin. The smooth, clean lines accented his strong jaw and the power he exuded. All the times I'd seen him before paled in comparison to how he looked tonight.

His eyes were glued to my back, which I knew was completely exposed in this dress. His nostrils flared and I smirked, It pleased me to know that his reaction to my cleaned-up appearance was as strong as my reaction to his. And he'd picked out the dress, so I don't know why he was so surprised. When you buy a dress like this for a girl, she's going to be showing a little skin.

Was this a date? We hadn't gone over that. I assumed he'd asked because he'd been too busy to find another date for tonight, but he'd also gone through the trouble of getting me all dolled up. It couldn't have just been a convenience thing, not after everything that had passed between us over the last few months.

"You look stunning," he said, grabbing the coat Rachel held out and helping me into it. I blushed and I pulled my hair up, so it didn't get caught and I swear I felt his breath ticking the back of my neck. The hairs there stood on end as I tied the coat's sash around my waist.

"Rachel, I trust everything will be okay tonight? You know how to get in touch with me if you need me," Rhys confirmed, keeping his eyes pinned to me.

"Absolutely, sir. Powering down right now," she said, turning her phone off. "Esme and I will have a great time. Enjoy the party!"

"I'll have to take you out like this more often," he said, guiding me into the elevator, his hand on the small of my back. The heat of his hand radiated through me as we stepped inside. As the doors closed, a predator replaced the polite Rhys of the past few weeks. Every spot his eyes lingered on made my skin heat even under my coat. As we drove to the gala, I felt naked although I was bundled up in a coat and tucked away in the back of the town car with him. My fingers toying with the seatbelt while I stared out the window, trying to pretend that I wasn't in a whole heap of trouble.

18

MEL

As we entered the museum, Rhys checked my coat and led me into the event. His hand that warmed me back in the apartment, set me ablaze as he settled it on the small of my back. His fingers were flush against my bare skin, making me hyper-aware of every bit of exposed skin and every inch of contact between us. I held my head high as we walked into the event space, which showcased various pieces of artwork. Heads turned as we made our way further into the room. My shoulders inched a little higher with each new set of eyes turned our way.

"Relax," he whispered, tickling my ear with his warm minty breath. "I would tell you they're not looking at you, that they're looking at me, but I know with you in that dress they are definitely looking at you," he said, plucking two champagne flutes off the tray from the waiter who had approached us. "Here you go. Don't let it go to your head," he said. I didn't know what part of tonight I shouldn't let go to my head. The fairy-tale makeover, him taking me out, the champagne, or the way he looked at me that made me want to drag him into an empty closet and beg him to end my misery.

But his remark cemented how much I didn't fit in with this crowd. I didn't know how to hold my champagne glass and my hands were super clammy for each embarrassing handshake, and the heels made me wobbly with each step. But his hand didn't leave my back for most of the evening. He guided me through the crowd, introducing me to everyone we met, smiles all around. With him leading the way, I relaxed. I smiled and tried to play my part as his date without falling on my face.

After a couple of turns on the dance floor, his face got closer to mine and he talked to me. Told me stories about a lot of the people in that room. Our whispered conversation, so private even though we were surrounded by a room full of people. He moved like a man who'd been born dancing, and all my worries about face planting out there were swept away as he used his firm, steady grip to lead me where he wanted me.

As the night wore on, the mystery of his world grew even bigger. People were talking mergers and acquisitions, golfing, yachting and every manner of things so far out of my league, I couldn't even comprehend that being my everyday life. Rhys was at ease, so in control of everyone around him. People deferred to him in almost every conversation. Waiting for his reply before they made up their minds about something and he took it in stride. I'd also never seen him smile so much before. This person he was in public was the one I remembered from the news stories and magazine covers, but he wasn't anything like the man I'd shared the same apartment with over the past few months. I wondered which side was the real him.

While the smiles were there for every conversation with

people who approached him continuously throughout the evening, every turn to me, every glance turned on the heat. The butterflies in my stomach were flapping their wings so hard they threatened to sweep me away.

"Don't drink too much champagne. I have plans," Rhys said against my temple as he was pulled away, nodding to the glass in my hand. The tingling of the champagne was pushed aside by the throbbing I felt from the promise in his voice.

I licked my lips in anticipation of what that might mean, his eyes were riveted to them. When he glanced up his eyes brokered no argument that tonight would be one I wouldn't soon forget. My skin flushed and I knew it wasn't from the drinks, but from the heat pouring off him. I needed to get out of there for a bit. Cool down before I made a complete ass of myself in front of everyone. I wandered out onto the balcony. The frigid air kept most people inside, but it was perfect for my overheated body. My breath was visible, floating in front of my face as I gazed out over the city, lights twinkling. Headlights and taillights looked like tiny dancing decorations coating the streets.

Goosebumps pebbled my flesh and I rubbed my hands up and down my arms, welcoming the air to snap me out of the haze I'd been stuck in. I needed a clear head around him as much as possible. It was so easy to let things get out of hand. And as much as I wanted him. Wanted to feel him. I had to keep my wits about me or he might completely decimate me.

"Do you want some company?" came a smooth voice from behind me, making me jump. I whipped around and stared at the man who'd entered my icy retreat. The tall blond stood a few feet from me, admiring the city, but I knew his attention was also on me. Whereas Rhys wore his tux with confidence and poise, this man looked like he'd beaten it into submission before putting it on. He was large where Rhys was lithe. His muscles strained against the jacket that had to have been tailor made for him. Maybe a professional athlete?

"I'm okay. It's a bit cold, I was just heading back in."

"Keep *me* company then. These stuffy parties can be such a bore, and I always feel so out of place," he said, standing next to me. I glanced through the doors to the balcony, where Rhys was still talking over whatever he'd been dragged away to discuss. And I knew all about feeling out of place there. Although I couldn't imagine this guy felt out of place. He might not have looked like he was born to wear one, but he certainly looked good in it. The black contrasted with his light blonde hair and striking blue eyes. If I wasn't already completely mindfucked by a certain green-eyed enigma, I might have been tempted by the man before me.

"Sure," I said, checking the doors again.

"Here, take this," he said, shrugging out of his jacket.

"No, it's okay," I protested. But he shook his head and put it around my shoulders.

"It's the least I can do if I'm asking you to stay out here with me." The warmth from his jacket immediately soaked into me, relaxing the muscles I'd tightened to keep the cold at bay. I wrapped the warm jacket around me tighter. The cold had settled in deeper than I realized.

"Thanks," I said, following his gaze out over the city.

"You're here with Rhys Thayer, right?" he said, peering over at me.

"Yes, I am." Nervousness bounced around my stomach, ping-ponging back and forth.

"I have to say, there's only a handful of things I've been

jealous of in my life, but when I saw you two walk in, I wished it was my hand resting on your back. His stare turned from playful to molten in an instant. It set me ablaze.

My breath came out in stuttered puffs. I didn't get the feeling this was just about me looking nice in this dress. Something was up, but I didn't know what. Power pulsed off him, nearly overpowering me. But it wasn't the same as it was with Rhys. This didn't make me want to drop my panties, bend over and beg for his attention. It made me want to run away.

"Thanks." I didn't quite know how to handle this. I didn't want to tell this guy off. I didn't want to embarrass Rhys. *Who knew who this guy was? A business associate? A potential client or something?*

"Killian," he said, extending his hand.

"Melanie," I said, placing my hand in his to shake, but then the shake stopped being just a friendly formality when he covered my hand with his.

"So where did he find you?" he said, running his fingers along the back of my hand. I shivered, this time not at all because of the weather. I had the feeling I had the starring role of a bug stuck in whatever kind of web Killian wove and I didn't know how to get out.

"I'm just the nanny. A last-minute person to come with him. He's been working really hard lately and I don't think he had time to find a real date." I tugged on my hand, but his grip was strong.

"I don't believe that at all," he said, his eyes roaming all over me.

"I don't know what to tell you. I'm definitely the nanny." I managed to tug my hand free from his grasp.

"Oh, I believe *that* one hundred percent, but I don't believe for one second that you weren't his first choice for a date. Rhys isn't known for letting anything slip through the cracks, so I'm sure he brought you here with a specific purpose in mind," he said, taking a step closer. I took a step back, my back hitting the stone railing.

"Listen, I'm going to head back inside. It was nice meeting you," I said, trying to step around him, but he sidestepped right along with me and I ended up banging into his chest.

"I'm sure there are all kinds of things you're able to do for him other than just watch his daughter, aren't there?" he said, touching my chin with his fingers. My first instinct was to jerk away, but I balled up my fist tucked in the sleeve of his jacket and was ready to deck him when Rhys swooped in and did it for me. The smack of his fist against Killian's face made me jump, nearly toppling over in my heels. He glanced over at me before he leaned right back into Killian.

As happy as I was for his rescue, the look on his face didn't spell out 'prince saving me from a villain' it was more like, "betrayed hero promising retribution." My stomach dropped as I watched him lay into Killian.

19

RHYS

Only something this important could have pulled me from Melanie's side tonight. When I had first seen her standing in the foyer, wearing the dress I'd chosen for her, it was all I could do not to tell Rachel to leave, so I could take Mel right there, up against the wall. But in that dress, I also wanted to show her off.

The past few weeks I'd been putting out fires and dealing with headaches left and right. This was the first night I'd been able to spend with Mel since the night in my office. That she was in the apartment had been good enough for me. She was there, safe under my roof. The temptation was so strong. I'd promised myself just a taste tonight. Just enough to take the edge off the need to have her.

Thomas, one of my fellow board members, pulled me aside. Rachel hadn't been able to get much information about the coup being staged against me, which was unlike her. She was usually up for a challenge and delivered every time. Thomas was a family friend, and his allegiance was stronger than most.

Thomas leaned in and warned in a hushed tone, "I

thought you should know. It's Killian Thorne. He's the one who's convinced everyone to hold the elections."

My blood ran cold at the confirmation of what I'd suspected from the beginning. Killian had had his sights set on me and my family for a long time. He'd fallen off the face of the earth after getting kicked out of school. Too proud to accept anyone's help, he left and we lost touch. Old friendship or not, he wasn't going to get away with this. It didn't make any sense to me. *Why was he doing this?*

"When did he approach the board?"

"A few months ago. He made it known that there was a scandal brewing with you and it would be in the best interest of our foundation to disassociate ourselves from you as quickly as possible. He said no amount of money would be able to salvage the reputations of anyone associated with you," Thomas said, whispering furtively.

"Did he say what information he intended to divulge?"

"No, not to me anyway, but whatever he shared with the rest was enough to get them to call for the election. He wants your seat," Thomas said. A flash of red across the room caught my eye. Melanie opened the doors to the balcony, and the frosty breeze made its way across the room to me. *She doesn't have a coat.* I needed to focus. Focus on the matter at hand.

"He's not going to get it," I said through gritted teeth. My blood pounded and my temples throbbed as I clenched and unclenched my fists. He thought he had the upper hand on me, but I'd be damned if I let his bullshit vendetta destroy everything I'd worked for and put my family in jeopardy.

"Perhaps it wouldn't be a terrible thing if you weren't on so many boards. I'm sure you'd like to relax, take some time with your daughter. You never took any time off after your wife died. I think maybe this could be a good thing," Thomas said, attempting to reassure me.

"I'd much rather have a hand in all the good work being done out there. You know how much I enjoy being at the helm, being able to direct what's going on with these foundations." Thomas smiled and nodded.

I played my part perfectly. I was the perfectionist, controlling billionaire who didn't want to see his money squandered. What he didn't know, what no one knew was that my parents weren't quite so sure I'd follow their do-gooder path in the event of their untimely demise. Every dollar I had was a result of the money I donated. I was required to donate a certain percentage to one of my charities. A charity vetted by the executor of my parent's estate. Only then would I get any money from the trust in advance of my full inheritance. Every cent ran through this bullshit of hoops and hurdles. Apparently, they didn't trust me. My parents would leave for months on end to be benefactors, heroes, even care givers to people all over the world, however their generosity and philanthropy ended the second they came back home, if and when they did. I was raised by a squadron of nannies. And I was a handful from the beginning. The nannies were as disposable as I was to my parents.

If I was kicked off the board, the money would dry up. I was afforded certain perks for my charity work, like my apartment, travel, hell even some of my clothes. Living the life of a billionaire, even a frugal one, came with certain expectations. Managing the expectations the world has of someone who has a trust fund as big as mine, as well as ensuring safety and security for Esme, meant my financial situation was carefully calculated. But Kill's interference could completely ruin all the plans I'd made. On my thirty-fifth birthday, which was only a couple of months away, the complete estate would be transferred to me without the strings. I'd finally be in complete control of my own life. But, if I didn't maintain those board positions, I got nothing.

"Thank you for warning me, Thomas. There's nothing Killian could reveal about me to create a scandal. I hope the board elections will be held without unsubstantiated rumors influencing anyone." My stomach dropped as I thought of the one secret I'd kept and would take to my grave. I lived my life in public, scrutinized and analyzed. I didn't want that for Esme. But if this got out, she'd never be able to escape what would rain down on us both.

"I'll be sure to tell them not to buy into whatever Killian is selling. I can't even believe he showed his face here today, wrangled a last-minute invitation," Thomas said, excusing myself. *He was here?* Tonight, was supposed to be a reprieve. A break from everything that went wrong in my life to focus on one of the things going right. *Mel.* I needed to get my hands on her.

Rubbing my fingers along the small of her back was a little game I played with her and myself. Each stroke, each caress a promise of what was to come later this evening. I wouldn't let the news Thomas delivered ruin my night, ruin the plans I had for her. Every phone call, meeting and trip I'd had to take recently put me further and further away from her and I didn't like it. Especially not after the taste I'd had of her already. But I could be patient.

I flung open the doors to the balcony and the scene unfolding in front of me made my blood boil. It took me a moment even to register who that was near Mel. Once I saw it was Kill, the man causing every nightmare going on in my life right now, I couldn't wait to get my hands on him. I stormed over to Melanie and Killian. He held her chin in his hand. His lips inches from hers. She wasn't his to touch. She wasn't even his to think about. She was no one's but *mine*.

I jerked him back by the shoulder and his eyes went wide as I let loose on him. The satisfying crunch of my fist connecting with his jaw echoed around the balcony, filling the winter air with the sound of my rage. My breath came out in heavy pants as I grabbed Melanie by the arm and swung her behind me. Kill stumbled back, toppling over, wiping the blood off his lip.

"And there's that Thayer control I've heard so much about. I knew you couldn't have changed that much since school. Nice of you to join the party, Rhys. I was having such a lovely conversation with Mel," he said, sitting up on the ground and spitting a mouthful of blood onto the granite. And then he did the one thing that made me want to wrap my hands around his throat. He smirked at me, his teeth a bloody mess. I wished I'd knocked a few out. I must be losing my touch. I stepped toward him and Melanie held me back. She grabbed my arm as I pulled it back, ready to deliver another set of blows.

"Rhys, don't," she said, holding onto my arm. She gestured with her chin toward the doors to the balcony. Other people from the gala stood at the doors, watching our display out here. Cage it. Push it down. Breathe. My normal mantra wasn't working.

"I'll be sure to let you know how those donations you've so generously made are spent once I have your seats," Killian said, dusting himself off and standing to face me. I lunged for him again, but Melanie held tight to my arm.

I glared at her over my shoulder. *What the hell was she out here talking to him about?* I'd deal with him first and then we'd be having a long conversation, which may or may not end with me fucking her so hard that she never thought of speaking to another man again. I glanced down at her and saw what was wrapped around her.

"Are you wearing his fucking jacket?" I seethed. Her eyes widened and she quickly threw it to the ground like a poisoned snake, wrapping her arms around herself. "Don't you come near her again. Do you hear me?" I roared at Killian. My control was gone. I grabbed her arm and stormed back into the gala. I didn't care who wanted to talk to me, I didn't have time for fake smiles and glad-handing. I called for Derek to bring the car around, as I hastily retrieved Mel's wrap and rushed her out the door.

The car pulled up in front of the museum. I guarded Mel's head as I helped her into the car. I tried to calm myself the best I could. The mask was almost gone now. She'd peeled it back and cracked it wide open by speaking to Killian out on that balcony alone. And now that I'd shown my true colors, she'd be sure to run. With that thought, I wanted Derek to turn the car around, so I could deliver another round of punishment to Killian.

If he'd screwed up what simmered between Mel and me, I wouldn't be able to keep myself from killing him. Nothing for me. Never anything for me. Everything was for everyone else. My money, my reputation, my work, even my daughter. Mel was meant to be the one thing just for me and now even that was in jeopardy. I was tired of waiting. Tired of keeping the reigns on tight. I had one goal. Exploring her body, spreading her out in front of me and finally being able to feast on her.

20

MEL

I have no idea what just happened. One minute I'm out on the balcony talking to some guy who obviously had a history with Rhys and the next, he's dragging me out of the gala, fuming. *Did he think I wanted to be out there with Killian? Couldn't he see the relief on my face when he got there?* Probably not since he was in blind-rage mode. I hadn't seen him like that before in public. He'd never let the dark side of himself out when other people were around. He'd saved that for me, in private heated moments where he made me forget how to speak and breathe.

"What were you talking to him about, Melanie?" he growled, his hand gripping my knee.

"Nothing. I was out there on the balcony. Then I got cold. As I was going back in, he came out and asked me to stay. To keep him company. He offered me his jacket and we had barely finished introductions when you came out." It was no use letting him know everything Killian said to me. With the way Rhys acted, he'd have Derek turning the car around so he could have another go at him.

"I didn't know who he was, and I didn't want to embarrass you by blowing off someone you might have business with. I'm not a liar, Rhys," I said. His suspicions agitated me. That he thought I was out there doing something wrong made me want to show him how wrong he was. Teach him a lesson about doubting me. But with his next words everything outside of the car ceased to exist.

"I will never do business with Killian Thorne and the only blowing you'll be doing is of me," he said, his grip tightening on my knee. His fingers made small circles on my skin. They traveled higher up my thighs as he gathered my dress and pushed it up higher. The look in his eyes dared me to stop him. Dared me to use the words, but I was at a loss. It was like the air had been sucked out of the car. The only things I could feel were his fingers and I squeezed my thighs together.

His warm hands slid between my knees, running the length of my thighs. Tingling pleasure flowed over me and my breath caught in my chest. He kept his eyes trained on me while his hands roamed. He got closer and closer to my panties. Each stroke up and down my legs, increasing the desire I had for him to move a little higher. The adrenaline from the end of our evening was still high and I was thrumming with energy. His fingers grazed my panties, drawing a gasp from me in anticipation of what was to come.

I didn't know exactly what he had in mind, but I knew I wanted it. The raw power from his fight with Killian still flowed through him. He was practically vibrating, though his hands were firm and measured along my skin. These past few weeks, every glance, every brush had set a simmer I thought I could ignore, but here in the car with him I couldn't ignore it any longer.

He tilted my head and ran his fingers along my neck.

"What were you talking about, Melanie?"

"I told you. Nothing," I breathed out, as his lips gently ran across my neck. His lips making of hyper-aware of every inch of flesh between my shoulder and my ear. This wasn't the sort of reaction I had expected when we left the gala. He'd been so angry, but this wasn't what I was used to when a man was angry. This was scary, not in a way that made me want to run and hide, but in a way that made me fear what things would be like after he was done with me. What I'd be like after he was done with me.

"Killian doesn't partake in idle conversation, Melanie. Everything he does has a purpose," he said, his hands running higher again, just skimming my panties. The red flush from my cheeks burned all over as he sunk his fingers in, rubbing against the crotch of my panties. I knew they were soaked through. I could feel it.

"I told you exactly what we talked about. I think he was trying to figure out why I was there. I'm sure I looked out of place," I said, my voice quivering as his hand dipped inside the thin elastic band of my panties. His lips trailed along my jaw and just a hairsbreadth away from my lips. I turned to him and his eyes burned into mine. I was lost, spiraling out of control as his fingers grazed my clit. I jumped and gasped as he massaged me, strumming my clit. My legs parted giving him easier access, but I maintained eye contact. It was what he wanted, what he needed and who was I to deny him?

"You are never to speak to him again, Melanie. Do you understand? He's not someone I want you entangled with, and I don't want you to get hurt." I bit back my retort that he was someone I probably should have stayed away from, but with his fingers parting my lips the words died in my throat. Then he threaded his hand through my hair. And his lips were so close to mine. His ever-present minty scent filled my nose along with the smell of my own arousal as his fingers continued their ministrations. My breath came out in small gasps. His full pink lips were so close to mine. This almost felt more personal than what went on under my dress, inside my panties.

He tightened his grip in my hair, the roots screaming for relief, but not me. I relished the edge of pain, better to keep me in the moment, not get lost and forget a single detail. And then his lips weren't just close, they were on mine, crushing my lips in a punishing kiss that was more like a marauding conqueror than the sweet and gentle kisses that people seeing him on TV might imagine he gave.

The heat in the car was almost unbearable on this cold winter's night. The windows steamed from the intense heat. Rhys pulled back from our kiss, his lips lingering on mine. I panted, eyes wide at what had just happened. My lips ached and his were twisted up in a satisfied smirk. He kept his hand in my hair, more gentle now, running his thumb along my cheek. My thighs trembled as his fingers continued their slow torment that made me shudder in anticipation of him possessing me, like he'd just done with my mouth.

"I didn't get my answer, Melanie. Do. You. Understand?" he asked, punctuating each word with a tap of his finger against my clit, making me jump each time.

"I wasn't doing anything. And where do you get off telling me who I can speak to? There was nothing going on out there other than me trying to be polite to someone at an event you brought me to." I might be someone under his control right now, unable to break away from the gravitational pull he had on me, but I wasn't going to let him rule my life. He couldn't tell me who I was allowed to talk to. That wasn't going to happen. Plus, I liked the little game we were playing.

"Don't make me repeat myself," he ordered, pulling back and tracing the seam of my pussy. I shuddered and a small moan caught in my throat. He was my weakness. I thought I'd had more than one over the years, but those paled in comparison to him. I wanted to rage against him, punch him in the mouth and tell him to fuck off, but I couldn't. I couldn't stop myself around him. He was too much for me to resist and I hated him for that. For allowing me to give over so much of myself to him.

"You will not speak to him again," he commanded, nipping my neck. I closed my eyes and rested my cheek against his head, all while his fingers stroked my clit before plunging inside me. I cried out then and gripped the seat beneath me. Suddenly, the slow build was completely out of control and I couldn't contain it any more. My orgasm ripped through me, shooting through my clit, racing up my spine and catching me off guard. Every part of me tingled, from the roots of my hair to the tips of my toes. I felt my pussy squeezing his fingers, not wanting him to let go. He gave me a few last pumps of his fingers, sliding in and out of my slickness as I shuddered, closing my eyes and moaning. He slid his hand out of my panties and brought his fingers to his lips. He sucked them into his mouth and another shudder coursed through me at the sight.

"Delicious," he said, closing his eyes and tilting his head back. When he opened his eyes, I knew I'd do anything for him in that moment. I wanted to return the favor. Needed to return the favor and I sunk to my knees in front of him. *Why was I doing this?* He was insane. I was insane. I didn't care that he bossed me around, trying to control me, hell that was probably what got me so hot in the first place. I'd never been one to give my power over to someone else, to let them lead, but with Rhys, he made it easy. He made it so easy that

I was drunk on the freedom of not having to think for a little while, even if I knew it would come back and bite me in the ass. Maybe with him, it would be a literal bite.

"No," he said, pulling me from my knees and up to his side, his arm around my waist. "We're home."

I glanced up and realized the car wasn't moving. Derek stood outside ready to open the door. *Oh my God.* I'd completely lost my mind, not even aware of what went on outside of the car. Outside of the little world we had created. I hastily shoved my dress down over my knees and tried to compose myself. I'm sure I looked exactly like I felt, like a woman pushed to her sexual edge by a man who could make a woman faint with just a smile.

Rhys hurried me into the elevator and up to the apartment, my heels in his hand. His fingers once again gravitating to the small of my back, as he led me into the foyer. His heated stare skimmed across my body. He pressed his body against mine and our lips were once again inches from one another when a scream and cry ripped through the air.

Esme came barreling down the hallway, Rachel hot on her heels. We immediately broke apart and crouched down as Esme launched herself into our arms.

"I'm so sorry," Rachel said, pushing her glasses back up her nose, wringing her hands.

"It's okay, Rachel. Don't worry. We've got it from here. What happened?" Rhys asked, glancing over at me. The simmer was still there, but the worry for Esme pushed that to the back burner—for now.

"I don't know. She was asleep. She went down really easily. Are you sure I can't help?"

"No, it's fine. We've got it," I said, rubbing Esme's back.

"What's wrong, sweetheart?" Esme's little arms tightened around both our necks and she shook her head. Rhys untangled them from my neck and picked her up, cradling her against his chest. "It's okay. I'm here. We're here," he soothed. Rachel hesitated before grabbing her bag and heading out.

"Esme, tell us what's wrong. We can't help, if you don't tell us," I said, as we walked down the hall, Rhys carrying her in his arms, and eventually laying her back in her bed.

"I had a bad dream about mommy," Esme said, her face shining with tears. Rhys's back straightened and he froze with Esme's hand gripped in his. The whoosh of the air leaving the room was palpable. Esme might have spoken to me, but she never talked about her mom. Never. I'd begun to wonder about her, but didn't want to pry and definitely didn't want to ask Rhys about it. The little searching I'd done online said she had an accident involving sleeping pills and died tragically. That was the extent of what I'd been able to find.

"Maybe I should go," I said, unsure which would make things worse, me staying or going. I stood and Rhys wrapped his hand around my wrist and shook his head.

"Stay," Rhys said, at the same time, Esme shouted, "No!" Well, I guess that settled that. I sat on the bed and grabbed her other hand.

"I had a dream about the bad man coming to take me," Esme whispered in little shuddering breaths. She squeezed my hand tighter. Something got to her and sent her into a panic. I looked to Rhys, who had his eyes closed, face tilted up toward the ceiling.

"Esme, the bad man is never coming for you. Never. I will protect you forever. You know that, don't you? I'll never let anyone hurt you." Rhys said so fiercely it raised goosebumps on my arms. Something had happened. Something had happened before, maybe what led Esme to stop talking.

He held her face in his hands and kissed her forehead. Esme nodded, gripping onto our hands until her breathing settled and she yawned.

Once she was asleep, Rhys tucked her hands under the blanket and left the room. I stood in the doorway looking after him, unsure if I should follow or not. I didn't know what happened to Esme tonight. I was overwhelmed with the desire to protect her sweet little heart. I just wish I had someone to protect mine.

I cautiously walked the path to Rhys's office, hoping we'd be able to talk about what happened with Esme and what happened back at the gala. My toes sunk into the carpet, each step like my legs were being weighted down with more lead.

I knocked on the cracked office door and peeked my head in. Rhys stood in front of the large windows, gazing out over the city, a tumbler in his hand.

"Rhys," I said.

"Mel," he replied, his back still to me.

"Do you want to talk about it, about what just happened with Esme? With us? Any of it?"

"No, I don't," he said, turning and setting the glass down on his desk. He looked up at me, his eyes radiating the pain behind them. I wanted to wrap my arms around him. "I don't want to talk about it because it's something I can't fix. It's something I'll never be able to fix."

"I'm sorry." I was at a loss for words. I didn't know what to do. I stood in the office doorway with the half-opened door behind me. "Do you want me to go?" I asked with my hand on the knob, ready to make a hasty retreat. Rhys glanced up and the fire was back in his eyes, causing my stomach to clench.

"No." He strode across the room and stood in front of

me. His hand came up and pushed against the door, closing it behind me. With his body, he pressed me up against it, breathing me in. My nose pressed against his shoulder, I inhaled his cologne, his musk. He reached behind my neck and undid the hook and eye at the top of my dress. His hand came up to my waist, sliding along my ass reaching for the zipper of my dress. I sucked in a shuddering breath. He gently pulled at my zipper as his hand traveled along my hip, every inch of me set ablaze by his hands gripping me, squeezing me.

He stared into my eyes as he pulled the top of my dress down. I broke out in goosebumps as the cool air hit my skin as he peeled the fabric lower and lower. With a final push over my hips, the dress pooled at my feet. I'd have to thank Rachel for the swanky panties. His nostrils flared as he glanced down at me. I struggled not to cross my arms over my chest. I held them at my side, willing myself to relax, but it was impossible.

He growled at my exposed nipples, pebbled from the cool air and my arousal. He dipped down, taking one of them in his mouth and I moaned, leaning my head back against the door. I threaded my fingers through his hair as his ministrations pushed me to the edge of a cliff I hadn't seen coming. Switching from one nipple to the other, he sucked, bit and tweaked them with his tongue before sinking to his knees.

Rhys looked up at me, his fingers hooked around the waistband of my panties, daring me to say no. I don't think I would have been able to even if I'd wanted to, and I definitely didn't want to. He slid them down over my ass. The scent of my arousal hit me, so I knew he knew what he was doing to me. I stepped out of my panties and he lifted my leg over his shoulder, parting my lips for him. I was completely exposed now. Completely open for him. He breathed in deeply before leaning forward, his tongue grazing my clit. I held my breath, afraid to breathe and break the spell woven over us and then he dove in, feasting on my pussy. I nearly toppled over, holding onto his shoulders to steady myself as he delved into me like a man starved.

My fingers dug into his shoulders as I leaned against the door, trembling as his tongue laved my clit, my opening, everywhere all at once. He pushed one finger into my pussy, pumping it in and out as I cried out. Then he added two more, sinking them into my pussy and I was gone. Set off like a rocket, everything went bright white for a second and my breathing stuttered in my chest.

He stood and spun me around, my breasts pressed against the hard, cool wood. "Grab the sides of the doorjamb," he grunted. I glanced over my shoulder, but he gripped my hair and turned my face back to the door. I rested my forehead there and stood on my toes to grab onto it. Then I felt him, covering my back. His weight pressing into me and I relished the crowding. My legs flush against his naked thighs. I tried to look back, but it was too tight to move. His hands reached in front of me and dipped back down to my pussy, spreading me open and massaging me again. His other arm came up and around my neck, tight enough that I couldn't move, but not so tight that I couldn't breathe.

Then he dipped his hips and slid his cock into me with one long hard stroke, every inch pushing deeper and deeper.

"Fuck, Mel." Was all he groaned against my ear. His chin, nestled in the crook of my neck, where he nipped at my skin. My head swam. It took my breath away. I was so full. And before I could bask in the pleasure coursing through me as he finally plunged inside to depths no one else had ever reached, he pulled out again and hammered right back in. His fingers continued to massage my clit, plucking and pulling me there. His head rested against my shoulder as he pumped into me, driving me higher and higher, so hard my feet came off the ground.

"So sweet," he moaned against my skin as I leaned into him, once again surrendering all my control to him, completely. Rhys flipped me around and wrapped my legs around his waist while plunging back into me. My back pressed up against the door and he held my face in his hand.

"Come for me," he demanded, cupping his hands around my ass, digging his fingers into my flesh and pounding his cock into me over and over. The angle had his stomach scraping against my clit with each thrust. My moans turned to gasps and his groans turned into grunts. My legs shook as my orgasm approached at lightning speed. Then he bit down on my shoulder, marking me, and I was gone. Flying higher than I'd ever felt as he bit out a curse and slammed into me a final time, holding himself there as he spilled into me.

21

RHYS

Mel. I rolled her name over in my mind as I wrapped my fingers around one of her curls. I'd fallen asleep with her last night, my arms wrapped around her. I told her about my past with Killian, about my wife, about almost everything. She listened quietly, running her fingers along my arms. I told her things I'd never told anyone, and that tight ball I always kept a hold on, never letting up, never letting go could finally be released. She showed me that I didn't have to be alone. I could be with her.

I'd slept without any nightmares, without any exhaustion, other than sexual. When I'd been with other women, even after a night of fucking, I still couldn't sleep. I'd have to burn off that excess energy in the gym, swimming lap after lap. With Mel, all I wanted to do was wrap her in my arms, tuck her head under my chin, close my eyes, and sleep. And that's what I'd done. I expected to wake up a few hours later, ready to battle my night demons, but when I opened my eyes, orange and red streaked across the sky as the sun peaked over the horizon.

I stared down at her. *Melanie Bright, what have you done to me?* I knew once I was finally with her it would change me. That's part of the reason I kept her at bay so long. Only allowing myself small tastes of her. But when I saw her on that balcony, wrapped in another man's coat, I couldn't stop myself. Screw restraint.

The urge to wake her was nearly insurmountable, but it warred with my desire to watch her sleep. Her hair fanned out across the bed, her arms up over her head. I traced the outline of her body with my fingers, goosebumps raising on her skin. She moaned in her sleep and turned on her side, inviting me to cover her back with my body. *Would she be able to do the impossible? Could I fall back asleep with her in my arms?* Something I never remembered doing with any woman, but something I thought was possible with her.

She was mine now. I was sure of it. More sure than I'd ever been of anything in my life. I couldn't let her go. I wouldn't let her go. She fit perfectly in my arms, around my cock and in my heart. I needed her like the air I breathed. I buried my nose in her hair and settled in.

Coffee. Was my last thought before I closed my eyes, my lids heavy, as sleep overcame me again. She smelled like coffee, even months after leaving the diner. It was like it had woven itself into her DNA. She smelled like coffee and comfort, and I wrapped my arms tighter around her, unsure if I'd ever be able to let her leave.

22

MEL

Waking up in Rhys's arms was second to none. I'd basked in the morning glow, glad Esme's interrupted sleep meant she hadn't been up at the crack of dawn as usual. I shot up in bed, but he pulled me back down.

"It's fine. She's still asleep," he said, against my neck. I didn't know how I felt about Esme finding me in her dad's bed, but he didn't seem concerned.

"What if Esme finds me in here?" I asked tucking the sheet tight around me.

"I'm sure she'd be delighted," he said, snuggling against my side. "Just five more minutes and then I have to get up." His eyes were still closed, but I couldn't deny him that, because it would have been denying myself, too.

Twenty minutes later, we finally rolled out of bed and joined the land of the living. We'd had another round in the shower, hot and sweaty under the cool spray of the water before getting ready for the day.

Rhys headed out to yet another meeting and I went to

find my favorite little girl. Once I tracked her down, Esme and I sat in the living room putting a puzzle together. We had almost completed it when the elevator door opened and Rachel stepped into the room.

"Hi, Rachel," Esme said, chirpily.

"Hi, Esme. Hey, Mel," she said, juggling tons of bags. I hopped up from the floor.

"Here, let me help you with those," I offered, grabbing some of the bags out of her hands.

"Thanks," she huffed out, completely out of breath.

"What is all this stuff? Where do you need me to take it?"

"It's stuff for the tree. Mr. Thayer...Rhys said to leave it here, the tree decorators will be here soon," she said, setting the bags down next to the ten-foot-tall tree that had been delivered earlier that day. *A tree decorator? Who knew that was a thing?*

"Hey Esme, do you want to decorate the tree?" I called over to her. She popped up immediately.

"Yes!"

"It's okay, Rachel. We can handle it."

"I don't know if that's a good idea. Rhys was quite insistent that the decorator would be here to do it."

"Don't worry, Rachel, I'll handle it. Just tell him it was my fault."

Ideas raced through my head on how to make this the best Christmas. And I was immediately transported to a time I'd hoped to forget, except for the fact that those memories helped me through so many hard times over the years. Since the night I saw Rhys at the pool, the nightmares as I called them no longer woke me in a cold sweat. I could enjoy them for what they were. And I looked forward to making even more happy memories, starting with this tree.

I'd never had a real tree for Christmas except for one year. I'd actually had two.

They brought me to Shannon three days before Christmas. The social worker's car pulled up in front of the small white house with blue shutters and a red door. I thought it looked like a house out of a story with its little flower garden out front and a holly wreath hanging on the door. My face pressed up against the cold window, my breath fogging up the glass. The Ashers came to the door and looked like the perfect mom and dad, like from a TV show. Shannon was wearing a pink apron and Ben had the paper tucked under his arm. I hadn't expected much. Anxiety and fear raced through my mind.

I had trembled as the social worker handed me off to them, my hand wrapped tightly around the garbage bag that held my meager belongings and that was it. I'd been left with these people I didn't even know. Other kids who waited with me for their placements told me all about the things they'd experienced. I was a foster kid now and while they seemed like nice people, when you grew up like I did and heard what I'd heard, trusting people didn't come easily. I cried myself to sleep that first night after Shannon left the room, after reading me three stories. I didn't know what to do.

It was so quiet. No beer bottles clanking, no loud music thumping. The only sounds were the wind outside my window, and the gentle hum of the heater turning on and off. My whimpers must have not been that quiet, as Shannon cracked open the door and peeked her head inside. I was so scared, I sat straight up in bed. It was never good to draw attention to yourself, never good to make an adult come into your room. But there was no yelling or screaming. No threats of what would happen if I didn't shut the fuck up.

She brought me a glass of water and set it on the table beside my bed. She stroked my head and hummed me a lullaby. I still remember the warmth of her hand and how soothing it felt running through my hair. My last thought that night was how much I wished I had a mom like her. And for a while I did.

The next few days were a blur of activity. They'd taken the decorations off the tree, so we could all decorate it together, complete with a string of popcorn wrapped around and around the whole length of the tree. Shannon had me help her wrap a couple of presents for Ben and we baked probably a thousand cookies. By the end of that week, I never wanted to see another cookie again, well not really, but for a solid twelve hours, I'd say I didn't want to have one.

By Christmas Eve, I was the happiest I'd ever been. I didn't even care about presents. Being there was the best present I could have asked for. Every night Shannon and Ben came in and read me a bedtime story. Watching them with each other showed me how things were supposed to be. There was no screaming and shouting, no one threw anything at anyone else, except for a pillow fight we had. Most importantly, no one was nodding out, so high they couldn't even form words. No needles and bent spoons laying all over the floor and counters. On Christmas Day, Shannon and Ben came to get me from my room and walked me downstairs.

"We've got a special surprise for you, Melanie. We hope you like it," Shannon said as we reached the bottom of the stairs. Last night, the tree had a few presents I'd helped Shannon and Ben wrap under it. I was so excited to see if they liked their gifts to each other. But when I looked under the tree that morning it overflowed with presents. They weren't for me. I learned a while ago, before I was seven, that Santa wasn't real. At least he wasn't real for kids like me, so I knew they bought them, but I didn't think any were for me. I'd have been more than happy to just watch them open theirs. I'd never had a Christmas like this before. It was like something out of the movies. I hadn't expected presents, so when they handed the one to me I was over the moon.

Grinning from ear to ear, I carefully opened the present. The wrapping paper was so pretty, I didn't want to tear it. I wanted to make it last. I hadn't ever gotten a present like this before. As I peeled off the paper, a grinning bear in a pink box stared back at me. The two of them stood in front of me, arms around each other, looking at each other like they'd never been happier. I couldn't hold back my smile. Ben took the box from me, opened it and held the bear out for me. I reached out and pulled my hand back, afraid this was all a trick for some reason. Even with all the kindness they'd showed me, I kept waiting for it to all evaporate and disappear.

"Mel, here. It's yours," he said, holding out the bear again. I took it from his hand and wrapped my arms around it, so tightly my arms ached. I'd never had a stuffed animal before.

"Are you ready to open your other presents?" Shannon asked, gesturing under the tree.

"Which ones?" I asked, so content with my bear, I couldn't stop staring at him. I didn't need anything else.

"All of them, silly" she said, pointing to the rest of the colorfully wrapped presents sitting under the tree. My mouth dropped open and I slid to my knees on the floor to get a better look at the gifts.

"All of them?" I asked. They both nodded and we spent the rest of the morning unwrapping the presents, drinking hot chocolate and eating pancakes. By the end of that day I had all the new clothes I could have ever wanted. New shoes. A new backpack for school. I don't think I'd ever had anything new in my life up until then.

That year hurt to remember. The keen longing that hits me whenever I think of my room. My bed, my clothes, my toys and most of all my parents, cleaves me in half and I feel like some part of me has been amputated without my permission. Like I can't breathe from all the tears that clog my throat, threatening to drown me under all I've lost. Skipping to school, waving to my mom from the backyard swing, snuggling up on the couch to watch a movie. It's all a painful reminder of the life I could have had.

We'd put the tree up again the next year just after Thanksgiving. I couldn't wait to help bake cookies and wrap presents again. I was in my room when I heard Shannon scream. She never raised her voice, never yelled. I thundered down the stairs and saw her in a heap on the floor, Ben crouched down to comfort her. The social worker was back, she'd popped in every couple of months at the beginning, but I hadn't seen her in a while. A pit formed in my stomach. No. I didn't want to believe it. No. They couldn't send me back. No. Ben and Shannon were my parents now.

And I knew it was all my fault. We'd gone out shopping for Thanksgiving. I wanted to ride on the pony rides outside the grocery store, but Shannon told me to wait, we could do it when we left. I was impatient, comfortable enough to disobey her now. She turned to pick up some things off the shelf and I decided I'd go on those rides by myself.

I just waltzed out of the store and onto the metal horse. I didn't even have any money to make it go, but I knew I deserved a ride on them. My life of deprivation slowly slipping away from me, I felt like of course I should get a turn. I want to yell and scream at myself. Go back in! Go back to her. But I didn't. The employees locked down the store, but I was outside. The police came and I'll never forget the sounds Shannon made when she ran over to me. It was like someone had died.

She held me in her arms and shook. I didn't know what was wrong, I just wanted to ride on the pony. I wrapped my little arms around her and breathed in her strawberry scent. She always smelled so good. With such a small decision from a little child, I completely changed my life. Imploded it without even knowing it.

One look at Shannon and Ben from the last step of the staircase and I knew. I knew I was going back. They couldn't keep me. My sadness transformed into anger. A ball of it welling inside of me, threatening to overcome me. Why? Why couldn't they keep me? Why were they letting them take me? I locked myself in my room and refused to come out. Ben had to unscrew the knob from the door.

The betrayal I felt when the door opened, like a gremlin trying to gnaw its way through me. Ben standing there with the screwdriver in his hand. That he would help them take me crushed me. I didn't care that his eyes were red rimmed and Shannon had her arms wrapped around herself leaning against the wall sobbing. I didn't care. They were letting them take me and that was all that mattered.

Each step down the staircase, with as much of my life that fit in my suitcase, was a step toward a place I didn't want to go. Bile rose in my throat as I stared back at Shannon and Ben from the social worker's car. It was my life story in reverse, but this time I knew it wouldn't have a happy ending. I think at some point I must have blacked out or stopped thinking or feeling. Because the next thing I knew I was back in my old house, in my old room, surrounded by everything I'd come to hate about it.

The stench of cigarette smoke covered with some floral scent. I could feel the holes in the mattress under the clean sheet Colleen threw over top of it. From the outside, it looked like she'd cleaned herself up, but I didn't trust it. I didn't trust her.

Colleen kept things nice for a while. The first few weeks when the social worker checked in, but it wasn't long before I came back from school and she'd gone through all my things. My bags ransacked, my belongings thrown on the floor, dresser drawers pulled out. She'd taken my clothes, my toys. I could only assume she'd sold them or traded them for money or drugs. Or hell, maybe she just threw them out to spite me. I stood in the doorway and it all came crashing down, I was back to being me.

It was months later that I finally snapped. I had to walk home from the bus stop. I didn't have a coat anymore. No umbrella to shield me from the pelting rain. Water soaked me through to the bone, as Colleen cackled and drank with her friends. My bear, the pink bear I'd hidden, so she wouldn't take, it sat out on the floor. His insides ripped apart. One of Colleen's friends had brought a dog with him, and it was busy tearing apart, and gnawing on my bear.

I stared at Colleen, my body vibrating with rage. I threw down my bag and launched myself at her. She turned to me, sluggish as always, moving in slow motion, and I wanted to claw her eyes out.

"Why did you bring me back? Why did you even want me? Why couldn't you have just let me stay?" I screamed at her as one of the guys pulled me off her and held me back.

"If I don't get to escape this life, sweetie, you sure as hell don't, either." Her eyes were glassy and hollow, and she threw her head back and laughed. Laughing at me and everything she'd ever done to me. I left, my anger no longer getting the better of me. I left and ran to the one place that I knew I'd be safe again. Only that didn't turn out the way I'd planned. It just broke me a little more.

23

RHYS

As the elevator door opened I was met with an aroma that immediately made me think of Christmas. It was a mixture of cinnamon, citrus, and cloves. At least that's what I imagined. My childhood had been much more austere. Less Christmas cheer and more paid companionship by a host of nannies while my parents were out saving the world. I don't know why they thought it would be a better idea to leave me behind than take me, but that's what they did. Almost every day of my life was spent on my own with people paid to look after me.

Not only was I overwhelmed by the delicious smells, but my ears perked up at the joyful music that danced through the apartment. It wasn't until I set my bag down that I realized the singing wasn't from the radio. It was from Esme. There they were. My girls. It hit me so hard, like a gut punch when I looked up and found them stringing a popcorn garland around the tree. Esme was so carefree and happy. Mel did that. She gave me back my little girl.

I stood and watched them for a while, so engrossed in their task, they didn't even notice me. The lights they'd already strung twinkled and the light bounced off the large windows in front of the tree. Mel had a chair pulled up tight to the tree and Esme handed her ornaments. Some of the ornaments looked homemade, like they'd just been made today. Tracings of their hands made to look like birds, something made of clay, and others that went along with the crystal and glass ornaments I'd had Rachel pick up earlier.

This felt right. I'd sent Rachel to get the ornaments I got every year. The ones my parents had for the photo ops of the perfect family in front of their tree. Looking at my girls now, I shook my head. I'd fallen into my parents' pattern again. Keeping up appearances, even in my own house. This was better. It felt better, like a real family. *Was that what we were now? Were we a family? Would Mel still be here, if I weren't paying her?*

Mel glanced over her shoulder and caught my eye. A huge smile spread across her face.

"You're home," she said. Esme turned and ran to me, jumping into my arms. Mel came over and wrapped her arms around me too. I breathed them both in. The two women in my life, I didn't care if Mel wouldn't be here otherwise. I'd think about it later. Worry about it later. Right now, I just wanted to enjoy this. The baggage of the day melted away when I had them in my arms, and I'd do whatever was necessary, to keep them there.

I had a feeling this Christmas would be better than any I'd had before. Growing up, I despised Christmas. Maybe that was why I preferred to keep it impersonal, mimicking the tree my parents chose. Everyone always thought Christmas must have been the most amazing thing when you had parents like mine. They were so generous, so loving, so caring. But no-one knew who they really were.

My parents' guilt and shame at how my father made his

money in the past, ate away at my father. It infected his mind and turned his altruism into a disease. One that robbed me of a childhood and of loving, caring parents. I was never allowed anything of my own. Every toy, every gift, every personal possession would be taken from me the moment they felt I cared too much about it. "Someone else deserves it more." "You already have so much." Those were the refrains of my childhood. And if I protested too much? I'd felt the sting of my father's hand more than once. So much for charity starting at home.

My closets were bare except for my school uniforms and three sets of clothes. When any of my nannies commented on my lack of toys, books, clothes or anything else like that, they were out, replaced by the next one. I'd sit in a barren room with nothing but a bed and a lamp and stare out the windows at other kids riding their bikes or jumping rope outside. My grandmother, perhaps sensing that something was amiss, gave me a book.

It was a standard children's book, nothing special about it, but it was everything. I cherished it. I read it every night, tucking it under my pillow when I went to bed. I had every line committed to memory. Every picture, every bend and crease of the book. It was the one thing that was finally mine. She would bake with me, spend time with me, she'd been the only one who seemed to care about me for just being me. And when she died it became even more important to me. She was the only one who truly loved me. The only person who never wanted anything from me other than a hug and some help cracking the eggs.

Every year the tree was piled high with presents, but I knew none were for me. My parents would take pictures in front of them and do interviews about all their good work. And it was the same every year, "Our son Rhys would like to donate every gift he's received to the less fortunate." I was fine with it, it didn't bother me at this point. But one year they brought in another child to accept a special gift I was to give away for a live Christmas special highlighting one year of the most generous donations from a single benefactor—my parents.

They handed it to me and brought me face to face with the little boy. He had scraggly hair, overly large clothes, but otherwise he could have been my mirror image. Same hair, same eyes, I smiled at him and he smiled back. Even then I knew how to play my part, but for him I was happy to give him something new.

Cameras trained on us, my mother handed the ornately wrapped present to me. The red and green bow sparkled with glitter and covered at least half the gift. As soon as I touched it, my hands trembled. I knew what was inside. I'd committed that book to memory, inside and out. Every aspect of it seared into my memory. I held it every day, read it every day.

"Give it to him. You must not be selfish. You already have so much," my dad said from behind me, his grip on my shoulder tightening. I clutched it to my chest and my father squeezed my shoulder so hard it made me whimper, but I didn't want to hand it over. It wasn't until he jabbed the bruise I already had under my shirt that I let go of it.

I held it out to the boy and watched him rip into the paper. Each tear exposing what I already knew. They'd taken it from me. I lunged without thinking and my dad grabbed me, jamming his fist into my back, bringing tears to my eyes. I bit my tongue so hard the salty taste of blood flooded my mouth, but I held back my tears. I know what would happen if I let one fall. You can't beat altruism into someone, but that didn't mean my father didn't try.

"You already have more than enough. It's not for you," he said. Nothing ever was. And that was the last day I lived with them. The last day I was home, not that there was much to go home to. They shipped me off to boarding school and I was still there when they died. Boarding school, where I could finally have some freedom, make friends and begin a life all my own.

When my parents died, people comforted and consoled me, offering their condolences for my loss. It seemed the world was mourning, but not me. People swore I'd be heartbroken. I didn't know my parents as the charitable and good-hearted people everyone else saw. To me, they had a sickness. Making money in weapons, strip mining impoverished countries had made them wealthy, but the court of public opinion and investors sentiments became too harsh on them. They changed their ways, which benefited the world, but changed them. They were so driven by the need to make up for what they'd done that I didn't even get a chance to have a real childhood. I was an instrument of their altruism, used to demonstrate how selfless they were. They'd withheld something that didn't cost a thing, their love and affection.

24

MEL

My morning went from bad to worse as I returned from dropping Esme off at school. The heavens opened and a freak hailstorm had started, pelting me with ice, four blocks into my nine-block walk home. Derek followed us to school in the car, but once I'd dropped Esme off, I'd told him to go on home. Stupid on my part for not checking the forecast. I dashed for cover under our building's awning. The doorman held the door open for me, but held his hand up to stop me.

"Ms. Bright, you have a visitor," he said, pointing to the far side of the entrance. My stomach plummeted. *Colleen.* She looked a hell of a lot worse than the last time I'd seen her. She looked to be down to her last few teeth. Her face was gaunt, with her scraggly blonde hair pulled up in a ponytail. She'd been pretty once. I still remember all the men who paraded through the house who thought as much. But those days were long behind her.

I shuddered to think I could have ended up like her. If it weren't for Shannon. I might have lived with her for only one year, but she was my mom. She was more a mom to me in that one year than Colleen had been in my whole life.

Even though Shannon and Ben broke my heart. Even though they didn't want me after all. At least I'd had my time there. My time where I felt like I was important. Maybe that was enough to save me.

I grabbed Colleen by the arm and dragged her around the corner. The last thing I needed was Rhys, Derek or someone else walking in and seeing her here. Me bringing my baggage into his life wasn't part of the deal.

"Looks like you finally got back to where you always thought you belonged, huh? Finally, found another rich family to take you in?" she said, as she stumbled to keep up with me. I ducked under the awning of a nearby shop and spun to face her.

"What do you want, Colleen?" I said, folding my arms across my chest. The sooner she spewed her venom, the sooner I could get rid of her.

"Can't a mother come visit her daughter in the big city? You never call, you never write. If I didn't know any better I'd think you didn't want to see me," she said, cackling, a cough overtaking her. She bent over, a coughing fit overcame her.

"I told you not to come. You wiped out my account. You should have more than enough. I even put some extra in there. You told me you lost the card to the account," I said, my eyes shooting daggers at her. She smiled slyly, putting her missing teeth on full display.

"I did lose it and then I found it again. And when I checked it, I found out you've been holding out on me. Always telling me you don't have any money. Nothing to give me. I'm your mother, damnit. I deserve some respect." That was the final straw.

"You think you deserve my respect? You think after all the shit you pulled when I was growing up that you deserve anything?" I asked, backing her up and out from under the protection of the awning. My hands shook and I tucked them tighter against myself.

"You always thought you were better, didn't you, especially after coming back from that family. Thought you deserved so much more."

"I thought I deserved clean clothes and food, Colleen. Any kid deserves that," I said, my voice going up an octave. She rolled her eyes. This was going nowhere. I needed her to leave. I needed her gone. *Now*.

"Why are you here? What do you want?"

"I need more money. I'm sure you have that now. You've got this big fancy job. Won't return my calls. Give me some money and I'll go away," she said, ducking her head as bits of icy rain pelted her.

"Fine. But if I give you this money, you leave, do you hear me? You leave and you never come back. I don't want to hear from you ever again. I don't want you coming near me. I want you gone." Her head nodded before I even finished my sentence. A part of me was sad that my own mother would agree to something like this, that she didn't even care enough to put up a fight. And the rest of me was so relieved that I'd never have to see her again. That I'd never have to look at her face and have it reflect back all the screwed-up crap I'd lived through.

"Fine, I can catch the next bus home, if you get me the money in two hours," she said, grinning.

Even more reason for me to hurry. She gave me the bus depot address across the river, and I told her I'd bring her the money. I hadn't spent much since I started working for Rhys. The paychecks were ridiculous anyway. I'd made more in a couple months than I'd made in nearly a year at the diner. Giving her some of it would set back my plans by only a couple of months. Plans I didn't even know if I'd go through with. I didn't know how long Rhys would keep me around. How long this thing between us would last. *What were we? What was I to him?* I didn't know yet and I was afraid to learn the answer.

25

RHYS

"Killian," I said, as I entered my office. Fucking prick lay on my office couch like he didn't have a care in the world. His arms rested behind his head and his feet were crossed at the ankles. He was the picture of relaxation, and I clenched my fists to keep myself from attacking him again. He seemed to relish it when I lost control.

I couldn't believe Rachel just let him into my office like this. Something was up with her lately and I didn't know what it was, but she seemed distracted and distant. Things were slipping through the cracks.

"Rhys, so nice of you to turn up. I've been here for hours," he said, taking his hands from behind his head.

"Maybe if you'd made an appointment, you wouldn't have had to wait so long. What do you want, Killian?" His visit was out of the blue, but everything Kill did was calculated, and pre-meditated. My temper flared.

I knew he was behind the board elections, but what I didn't know was why.

"I have a proposition for you that I'd like you to consider," he said, standing from the couch and plopping down in one of the chairs in front of my desk. He unbuttoned his suit jacket and leaned forward, a big smile on his face.

"I'd like to talk about how we can get you out of this little board-election situation." His smug smile almost had me vaulting over the desk to wrap my hands around his neck, but I needed to get to the bottom of this and find out what his motive was.

"And what situation would that be?" My self-restraint creeping up to my limit.

"Cut the shit, Rhys. I know all about the stipulations of your parents' will. I know that you're going to get nothing if you don't sill hold your current board positions on your birthday coming up. But that's not why I'm here. I don't give a shit about that. I'm here for justice, for Beth."

"What the hell are you talking about? Justice for what?" I fumed. He was a man I considered a friend and it came back to bite me in the ass. *Justice?*

"Oh, I think you know there's a lot more at stake than just your bank accounts. I don't think you want anyone to find out about what you did to Beth," he said, rage pouring off him in waves.

"What I did to Beth? I did nothing, but try to provide the best for her. I did everything I could to keep her safe. I tried to help her." I slammed my hand against the cold glass of my desk, so hard my knuckles throbbed.

"Helped her right into an early grave," he said, his teeth clenched.

"You have no idea what the fuck you're talking about." The muscles in my neck were so tight, I was afraid something would snap. He didn't know anything about it. How hard I tried to keep her away from the drugs. How hard it was to live with someone who'd lie through her teeth to get her next score. Put her own daughter in danger chasing after a fix. She'd been from the same neighborhood as Killian and never felt like she fit in in my world. Maybe part of that was my fault, but I did everything I could short of chaining her to the bed.

"And you think the boards are going to have an issue with Beth's drug addictions? You think they are going to let go of the steady money that gets deposited to every one of the charity bank accounts? I did everything I could for Beth. I tried so hard to help her stay clean. I've been playing this game for a long time. I'm disappointed in you, Killian. I'd have thought someone like you would have had a much better plan than that. Come on," I said, dropping into my chair. The tightness in my chest ebbing away just a bit. If that was his ace in the hole, then screw him and his empty threats.

"I'm not talking about Beth's addiction, I'm talking about her murder," he said, his eyes blazing, fury churning just as deeply as mine.

"Murder? Really? Why would I murder Beth?" I said, trying to keep my voice level.

"Maybe she didn't fit in with your perfect plan for your life? Maybe you couldn't handle that she preferred Allan to you?" he growled.

"You're out of your fucking mind. *Get out!*" I ground out, my jaw so tight, my teeth ached.

"Beth didn't die in your apartment. She didn't die like you said she did," he said, crossing his arms over his chest. My face went pale, as the blood rushed from my head. Suddenly I realize I've been taking the ability to breathe for granted my entire life. Because right now, I'm in a vacuum completely cut off from everyone and everything but the pounding panic that's racing through my body.

"Who said she didn't die in the apartment?" I clear my throat and try to maintain my composure.

"I do. I've seen the real police report. The one you tried to have buried."

"Get the fuck out of my office. You don't know anything about my life or anything about what you're talking about." My mind raced, trying to figure out where the hell he'd gotten that report. Had I covered up what happened to Beth? Yes, but I never would have hurt her. I did everything I could to save her. Everything to save her and protect my daughter. But I didn't need the news floating around about what really happened to her. Or people asking questions about Esme's having been there.

Killian glared at me and it made my blood boil. I balled my hands up into fists, my knuckles turned white as I planted them on my desk to keep myself from vaulting over it and smashing his head in.

"I thought all those years ago we promised we wouldn't lie to each other? You know she didn't die that way, and I know it, too."

"No one will believe your lies."

"They aren't lies and you know it. And it just so happens that I know someone who was there. Someone who knows all your dirty little secrets and someone who can't wait to bring you down," he said, pushing up from the chair and leaning against the desk. I bared my teeth, holding myself back.

"Why are you doing this?"

"Your parents stole my legacy from me. It's only fair I return the favor. Your fall from grace will be so satisfying. Maybe now everyone will know just the kind of man you are. Enough with the façade, Rhys. Let the real you out," he said, spittle falling on the desk between us. My control snapped. My future was in jeopardy. I wanted him to feel an ounce of the pain that shot through me. I tackled him to the floor, my fist smashing into his face. Like an out-of-body experience, I threw myself across the desk. His eyes widened. He knew of my restraint, but he didn't know just how far he'd pushed me.

It wasn't just me he threatened, it was the people closest to me and I wouldn't let anyone get away with it. Especially not him.

He grabbed me by the collar, ducking his head out of the way of my fist, which hit the floor. Pain exploded in my hand and radiated up my arm. He flung me off him and landed a solid punch against the side of my head. My vision swam and my ears rang as I blocked his next punch and landed one solidly in his stomach. He doubled over and wheezed, putting his hand on the floor to steady himself. Blood dripped from his face onto the floor and he wiped his mouth with the back of his hand, his teeth bloodied. He raced at me before I could react and, lifting me up, he slammed me down on my glass desk. It shattered under our combined weight and we were both showered with shards of glass.

I groaned and rolled to my side. Killian braced his hands on the floor, small rivulets of blood covering his palms, and pushed himself up.

"I didn't think you had it in you, Rhys. I thought all that talk about control was just the pussy's way out of a fight, but look at you. Getting down and dirty with the peasants."

"You threaten my family. I'll fucking end you," I said, seething. My fists clenched and unclenched.

At the sound of all of the commotion, Rachel burst into the room, her eyes wide with terror and her mouth wide open.

"Oh my God," she said, her hands covering her mouth. "What did you do?" she shouted at Killian.

"I told you not to disturb us," Killian said. I pushed myself up off the floor.

"You just said you wanted to talk. That you had something important to tell him. What the hell, Kill?" she shrieked. I quirked my head to the side. *Kill*. I didn't know many people that called him that. Especially not someone who'd only met him in a professional capacity. And Rachel was never so unprofessional as to call a guest of mine by their first name. And then it hit me. *She knew him!* Not in passing, or because of the digging I had her do. *She knew him.*

"You're working with him?" I said, storming over to her. "You've been reporting on me to him?"

"What? No, please, Mr. Thayer. It's not like that at all. I would never break your trust like that. I haven't told him anything about you." I didn't take betrayal lightly. Rachel was more than an assistant. She'd been my right-hand. She'd been in my house. Watched my daughter.

"You're done! Leave!" I shouted. Tears formed in her eyes, but I didn't care.

"And get the fuck out of my office," I roared at Killian.

"Gladly," Killian said, bowing. He reached out to touch Rachel's arm and she flinched away. "You know where to find me," he said to her before striding out the door like he didn't have a care in the world. And he didn't. He'd just destroyed my entire world. I turned my icy glare back to Rachel. *In my own house.* I shook my head. It looked like I had lost my touch. Here I thought I didn't let things get past me. Sure of everything happening around me. And she was right here under my own nose.

"Get out," I seethed. I couldn't even look at her.

"Please, Mr. Thayer, it's not like that at all. I'm not working for him. I never have been. He only asked to wait in your office. Said he had something important to tell you and he didn't want to do it in the lobby. I didn't know he had anything like this planned," she said, her voice quivering and motioning to my destroyed office.

"I said get out," I roared. She jumped and scurried out the door. I ran my hands through my hair and let out a primal scream before storming out. *I needed to fix this. I needed to fix this now, but how?*

26

MEL

I rode the elevator up to the apartment, running inside to grab my wallet before running back out. Derek stepped aside as I rushed into the elevator with a box in his hands. I didn't even stop to talk, I waved and he waved back. I'd stopped at the bank to get Colleen's money. I filled out the withdrawal form and went to the teller. She handed me back and envelope, which I tucked safely in my pocket. I glanced at the receipt the teller gave me and stumbled. I raced back up to the counter.

"Sorry, there's something wrong," I said, sliding the paper across the counter. "My balance is way wrong," I said, jabbing my finger at the *Available Balance* line. "While I would love to have all these zeroes in my account, they don't belong to me." I'd heard enough stories about people going out of their minds and spending money like crazy when something like this happens and then promptly going to jail.

"Are you sure?" she asked, her keyboard clacking as she typed away.

"Completely. As much as I'd like it to be, this balance is definitely not mine."

"It's not a glitch. Not that I can tell. There was a deposit made in your name earlier today," she looked up at me expectantly, like it would have just slipped my mind that someone deposited the wealth of a small nation into my account.

"Made by whom?"

"It says it came from Thornton-Smith."

"I don't know who the hell that is. And this isn't my money." I checked my phone for the time. I needed to get this money to Colleen now. I needed to get her out of the city now. Then I could deal with whatever the hell happened here. "Can you have someone look into this? I need to get it fixed."

"Okay, Ms. Bright, I'll have someone look at it and give you a call."

"Okay, thanks." I said, rushing out of the bank and heading across the river to the address Colleen gave me, carrying more money than I'd ever had in my life, tucked into my bag. *Please don't get mugged.* "Please don't get mugged." That was my mantra as I hopped off the train. Colleen sat leaned up against the wall of the bus terminal, smoking a cigarette, blowing a cloud of smoke over everyone who passed by.

"Here," I said, shoving the envelope at her. "It's all there. Take it and leave. This is it. I don't want you coming here again."

"Why thanks, daughter of mine. You got that pretty quickly, maybe I should have asked for more," she said, laughing at a joke that was only funny to her. My hatred for her ran deeper than anything I'd ever experienced, more than anything I ever want to experience. Because if someone or something could generate more hate than I had for Colleen, I'd better be dead or they'd be.

"Colleen," I warned. I didn't need her making a habit out of this.

"Fine, fine. I don't want to come out here again anyway. You never appreciated the things I did for you. Always so ungrateful. If I'd known you were going to be such a hassle, I'd have let those uptight assholes adopt you when they wanted to," she said, stubbing her cigarette out on the wall and flicking the butt on the ground. My mind froze as I processed her words. *Adopt. Me.*

She pushed off from the wall and walked toward the buses. I couldn't move. Everything that happened to me after I left my home with the Ashers flashed through my mind. Every night going to bed without food. Every tease and taunt because of my dirty clothes, every night I locked myself in my room because of the way Colleen's many visitors stared at me. And worst of all, the day I ran away, after finally figuring out where Shannon and Ben lived.

I wasn't more than eight when I had yet another visit from a case worker. Even after all that time, I still wanted to go back. I missed them, even though the betrayal burned bright. I knew if I could just see them again they would fix everything. I begged anyone who would listen to let me go back, but the court ruled that my mom was a fit parent. She told them everything I said was all lies, the ravings of a child who just didn't want to live with her. They branded me a liar and a troublemaker.

Since I'd slipped away from Shannon that day and the police had been called, I was not to be placed back with them. What a load of crap that was. During our meeting, the social worker stepped out to take a call, and I glanced at my case file sitting on the table. I checked the door and flipped the folder open. Flipping through the many, many pages in the file I found what I looked for. I found the address. I scribbled it down on a piece of paper and closed the folder.

I looked up the address when I went to school and figured out how to get there. Two buses, followed by a three-mile walk in the pelting rain, and I was back at the house. *My home.* Peacefulness settled over me. Even in the freezing rain I was happy. It was like everything would finally be okay. I'd finally be okay. I knocked on the door and music drifted out from the kitchen. I slipped around the side and peeked in the window. Shannon was singing off key as she always did, standing in front of the stove. Ben came walking in with a mug in his hand and gave her a kiss.

I smiled, even out there in the freezing rain it made me so happy to see it hadn't all been in my mind. *It was real. They were real.* I lifted my hand to knock on the glass, when a blur came racing into the kitchen, jumping into Ben's arms. He put his mug down and picked her up. A little girl. Another little girl. *It was too long. I'd been gone too long.*

Pain sliced through me like I'd been run through with a knife. It hurt deep down in my soul, like someone ripped away the last lifeline I had as a drowning victim. I don't know how long I stood out there, but it was long enough for me to be soaked through and frozen to the bone. I don't even know if it was the rain that did it. *I'd been replaced.*

My life had been taken over by someone else, and now all I had left was the one I was running from. It would never get better than this. I'd made one mistake, one little thing that sent ripples through my life and the lives of everyone around me and destroyed it all. Smashed it into a million small fragments that couldn't be put together again.

As I stood there, the chill of the air was nothing compared to the icy barbs I shot at her. I stared at Colleen, feeling like it was a lifetime ago that I'd run from her, never wanting to look back. She stood in front of me as the broken woman who gave birth to me gloat that she'd ruined the one good thing I had when I was growing up. The fire burned in my eyes as tears formed and pooled. Her head whipped around so fast, it wasn't until the sting traveled up my arm, burning my palm, that I realized I had smacked her.

"Don't you ever speak to me again," I said, my voice full of venom and anger. "You are not my mother. You've never been my mother. And I swear, if I ever see you again, I'll kill you." I shook with so much rage, I didn't know how I could walk straight. I longed to be back in my bed. No. I wanted to be back in *his* bed. Back in Rhys's bed, in his arms, because there I felt like all things were possible. Like the world wasn't a horrible place and like I finally belonged.

27

RHYS

After Killian left, I went out. I pulled the collar of my coat up high as I stepped out into the blistering cold. Sharp bits of ice pelted me in the face as I staggered out into the eerily quiet street. I couldn't think straight. Derek joined me at some point. I don't even know when. He fell in step behind me. His presence was like a guard watching over a prisoner. *Deadman walking.* That's what I felt like right now. I didn't know what to do, but I wanted to see Mel. No. I needed to see her.

I walked all the way back to the apartment, numb, as I stepped into the elevator. Derek took up his post in the lobby. The door had almost closed, when Mel showed up in the lobby, shaking the sleet and snow from her hair. A smile tugged at my lips. There were only a few things that could bring a smile to my face right now, and she was one of them. I held the door open for her.

"Hey," she said, smiling back at me. She seemed upset. Her eyes were ringed with red. It seemed we'd both had a shitty day.

"Hey," I said, back, pushing her hair back behind her ear. "Do you want to talk about it?"

She shook her head and stared back at me, touching on the small cut above my eyebrow. I winced, having forgotten it was there.

"Do you?" she said, nodding toward me. I shook my head.

"Good," she said, pressing her body against mine and pulling my head down, our lips meeting. The freezing coldness of our skin slowly seeped away with the fire brewing between us. It had been too long since I had her in my arms. Since I felt her wrapped around me.

"Mel," I moaned, as I broke off our kiss. She buried her face in my collar.

"I need you, Rhys. I just need you," she said, refusing to look up.

"Then you're going to have me," I said. The elevator opened. I picked her up, wrapping her legs around me. I rushed her into the apartment and leaned her up against the small table in the foyer. I shrugged off my coat and pulled hers off. She fumbled with my belt buckle, undoing it as I worked on her jeans. I slid them down over her ass, jerking her forward so I could pull them off. They dangled from one foot, her shoe still on. I took out my cock, not even stopping to stroke it. I was beyond hard. Whenever I was with her, I was always hard. I slid into her, bottoming out, catching her moan in my mouth as I tasted her sweetness.

She hitched her leg on my hip, her jeans jangling behind me as I slammed into her. The table rocked and swayed with each thrust. She gripped my shirt in her hands, fisting the fabric as I reached down and slid my fingers across her clit. I strummed it and then her legs tightened around me, her pussy so tight, I could barely move and she came, screaming my name against my neck.

I followed her over the edge, filling her with come as my legs nearly gave out from under me. Her pussy still milking me as the two of us stood panting in the middle of the foyer, almost completely clothed. I gradually came back to myself. Feeling in my arms and legs returning as she hopped down and fixed her clothes. We had a lot to discuss.

I grabbed the police report out of the safe and put it in Mel's hands. She flipped through it, digesting everything inside. The truth of that night in the rest stop. The truth of why Esme stopped speaking. Other than the officer there, Derek and I were the only people who knew about it. And now Mel.

"You don't understand. I can't just allow whatever Kill's planning. He knows something. He knows something that could destroy everything," I said, running my hands through my hair. The threads were beginning to unravel. After a shower, I brought Mel back into my office and told her about my afternoon run-in with Killian. I knew he was an asshole. Hell, I was an asshole when I wanted to be, but I had no idea the depths he would go to just to get at me. And there was Esme caught in the crosshairs. I couldn't let anything happen to her. I'd kill him first.

"Rhys, what does he know?" *Could I tell her?* The people who knew my secret could be counted on one hand, hell, on two fingers.

"It doesn't matter. He's going to try to use it against me, but I'll leave before that happens. I'll pack up and we'll leave. The three of us. We can go somewhere. Disappear and start over," I said, grabbing onto her hands. If this got out it would destroy the life I'd tried to build, but if we were together, maybe we could weather the impending storm.

"Now you're starting to scare me. What could he know that you are so afraid will get out? Is it something illegal?"

The day my wife died. The day they laid my little girl in my arms. The day the test results imploded my world. And then it didn't matter. What mattered was keeping Esme safe.

"It's not something I want to get out. I don't want Esme to know. I don't want her to ever doubt how much I love her, and I won't let anyone take her away from me. I don't care whose she is, but she's my daughter and that's all that matters," I said, vehemently. This was a declaration I'd made the day I found out and would make until the day I died.

28

MEL

And then it hit me, like a grand piano pushed from the thirtieth floor. My stomach lurched and the picture became crystal clear. How much more important all this was, than just some board election. It wasn't about the money or reputation or any other bullshit. It was about Esme.

"She's not yours," I whispered. A plunging sensation overwhelmed me, like I'd been thrown up in the air and came crashing back down. Everything tunnel-visioned around me. Rhys rounded on me with more fire in his eyes than I'd ever seen before and a mixture of so many other emotions.

"She is mine. She is mine in every way that counts," he shouted, but then his shoulders rounded and he splayed his hand across his forehead. "But biologically, no. She isn't. I didn't find out until she was almost one," he said, grabbing a glass off the bar and pouring himself a drink.

"How did you find out?" I sat on the edge of his desk, gripping the sides so tight my knuckles turned white.

"She was out playing in the park. Beth was supposed to

be watching her. She took a nasty fall. We rushed her to the hospital and they didn't know if they'd need to do a blood transfusion, so they recommended I go down and give some. I'm O-negative. My wife was O-negative. Esme is A+. It's genetically impossible. And then I had a paternity test done," he said, gulping down the amber liquid, his Adam's apple bobbing.

"My loving doting, junkie wife," he said, throwing the glass against the far wall. It exploded with shards flying across the room. I didn't even jump. I was numb. This was a secret he'd held for years, something he'd lived with every day. The idea that someone might find out. Someone might take her from him.

"Someone knows," I said, my stomach dropping.

"Yes, someone knows. Killian took it upon himself to do a little digging. Wants to expose me for the fraud I am, but what he doesn't realize is that he unearthed something far worse. Something I've dreaded since the day I found out the truth."

"She's your daughter," I said, vehemently. She was his in every way that mattered. "You can't let anyone take her," my voice raising up an octave. The room swam as my breathing increased. They couldn't take her. He couldn't let them take her. My vision blinked in and out and my chest constricted like someone was crushing me. I could barely breathe. *What the hell was happening to me?*

Then he was there, in front of me, holding my face in his hands. Tears prickled the backs of my eyes. They couldn't take her away from him. What kind of father would they even be sending her to? A shudder ripped through me.

"Mel," he said, standing right in front of me, but it sounded like he was a mile away.

"Mel!" He shook me and a ragged sob ripped through

my chest. I buried my head into Rhys's shoulder. They couldn't take her away from us. His strong arms wrapped around me, holding me up when all I wanted to do was sink into the floor and disappear. *Was this how my mom felt when they came for me?* My real mom, she might have only been in my life for a year, but it was the best year of my childhood. *Shannon*. I can still smell her warm strawberry smell and see her bright smile. And then she was gone. Forces beyond my control ripped me away from her and threw me back to the wolves.

It was almost cruel. To get a glimpse of what could have been. What my life could have been like if I hadn't been born to Colleen. But those memories were a lifeline I needed so many times growing up, like a girl who dreamed she was a princess who waited for her parents to come back and claim her. My sobs grew louder and my fingers dug into his shoulders as I wrapped my arms under his. *Please don't let this be happening.*

"Mel, don't worry. They won't take her away. I won't let them. I'll do whatever it takes," he said, pressing his lips to mine. I grasped onto him like a lifeline as my life story replayed in front of me in excruciating detail. I should be the one holding him up, comforting him. But I was a wreck, I couldn't imagine watching them walk in and take Esme away.

Derek walked into the office like I wasn't even there. No head nod or anything.

"You're going to want to see this, boss," he said, handing a tablet to Rhys, along with a stack of papers. I leaned forward in my seat. He glanced at the tablet before scrolling across the screen and dropping it onto the desk. The energy in the room shifted. *What the hell was on the tablet?*

"You took money from Killian?" Rhys growled, glaring at me.

"No. No, I didn't," I said, trying to piece together what was happening.

"Then what do you call this?" He held the tablet up and right there, on the screen in living color was my bank account. Extra zeroes and all.

My heart stopped. *How did he know? How the hell had he gotten into my bank account?* I'd been trying my best to figure out where the money came from, and the bank had been beyond useless, but now it all fell into place. I shook my head. This couldn't be happening.

"I didn't, Rhys. I swear to you I didn't. The money just showed up in my account."

"When?"

"Today. It completely slipped my mind with everything going on. I didn't even know it was him. I didn't know what was going on," I said, hoping he would believe me. I should have told him, but with everything going on, there wasn't time. I figured the bank would figure it out, take the money back and case closed. I didn't plan on spending it. It wasn't mine and I forgot about it.

"Are you sure it wasn't for services rendered? First Rachel, then you. I've been so blind. Stupid to fall for your tricks. You must have all had a good laugh at how fucking stupid I am."

"Rhys, it isn't like that. I haven't met Killian except for that once at the gala. That's it. I don't know why or even how he would deposit money into my account."

"Maybe to help him make the case for why they should take Esme? Get as much insider information as he needed to destroy me and take her away? But I'm not going to let anyone take her."

29

RHYS

When Derek showed me the tablet I couldn't comprehend what I saw. It didn't make sense. Why would she have had this kind of money deposited into her account? And then it dawned on me. She wouldn't, not unless Killian got something in return. I'd told her so much about myself. I'd spilled my guts and opened old wounds to her and she hadn't told me much about herself. I didn't know much more than what was in her file Derek gathered for me. *Did I even know her? Was everything I felt, just me playing pretend?*

My heart pounded in my chest, like it was trying to escape. Trying to run away from what this meant. Killian would have to get something substantial. But it was the folded letter that nearly sent me to my knees.

A letter from a lawyer demanding a paternity test. They had to be connected, there was no way they couldn't be. I looked up at the woman I'd opened my heart to, the woman I'd just been inside. I saw nothing but a viper. I didn't want to believe what I saw, but how could I doubt it? She disappeared today, Derek saw her leave. She has a mountain of cash deposited into her account and now this. A demand for me to submit to a paternity test.

Everything I've worked for every day. To keep my little girl safe, to protect her from where she could have ended up with a dead mother and a junkie father. And now it was all crashing down. It would all come out. Every single thing I'd tried to hide. The past reared its ugly head and Mel was at the center of it all. I shoved the letter to her, wanting her to see the ugliness that she brought into my life.

"That was him in the park, wasn't it?" she asked, playing her part perfectly.

"Of course, it was him. And what type of coincidence is it that you come into our lives and he shows up. Did Killian contact you and tell you to bring her out there? Did you think he'd just be able to take her?" She shook her head and tried to speak, but I didn't want to hear her denials. "You were using me, just like everyone else." I couldn't breathe. I thought she loved me. I thought if anyone could love me for who I was, it was her, not for what I could do for them or give them, just my love. It hadn't been enough for my parents or anyone else I knew. I thought she was different.

"Rhys, I'm not lying. I'd never lie to you about something like this. I...I love you. I love Esme," she said, tears in her eyes. *Love.* I rolled that around in my mind. I thought I loved her. I'd been so ready that I put my daughter at risk. The one person who loved me more than anything. It was my fault. I let her in.

I had enough to deal with. Enough to handle. Enough to protect and I wasn't going to be pulled even deeper into her web. I'd finally let myself feel. Let myself get comfortable that she was mine, finally mine and now she would rip that all away from me. Help them take my little girl.

"You played me." The veins in my neck throbbed and I hung on by a thread.

"I haven't. I wouldn't. Why would I do that?"

"Because of the payday Killian promised you." *Was she screwing him, too? Like Rachel? Was any of this real?* My mind raced as I tried to make sense of everything.

"I would never. I've only met him once. I haven't had anything to do with him."

"Get out," I roared. She jumped and blanched under my glare. *Good.* I gritted my teeth. She'd lied. She wasn't mine at all, she was like every other user who'd ever danced their way into my life. But this time I'd extended the invitation. I let her do this to me. Mel's lip quivered, and I chained up my heart and closed my eyes. The control slid back on, like a warm comforting coat.

"I would never do anything to put her in jeopardy," Mel pleaded. "I'd die before I let anything happen to her. The fact that you don't believe me. That you don't trust me shows me you're not thinking straight. You're doing this because you're scared. You're scared because what we have is something neither of us have experienced before. You don't think I'm scared? That I know which way is up around you? That the thought of losing Esme makes me want to wrap her up and run out of here with her?"

"Do you know how I knew you wanted to do that? Because the same exact thought ran through my head. The minute you said it."

I can't look at her. This is what she and Killian planned. Maybe trying to wring a bit more out of me.

Mel sniffed, wiping at her face with her sleeve and choked out, "You're going to realize you were wrong. You're going to see how much hurt you've caused us both, just because you couldn't face the fact that I love you. That I love

Esme. I would never hurt either of you, but if you can't look past your past, then it will never work."

I didn't care about her pain, I can't care about it. The fate of my little girl hung in the balance. I don't know why I thought things would be different. That she could return the love I had for her. My selfishness created this mess. She dug that knife in deep, her scent lingered on my skin and I wanted to scrub it off.

"Leave Mel, there's nothing left for you to take now. You've taken it all."

30

MEL

The roar in my ears disoriented me as I tried to figure things out, clear my head. Rhys thought I wanted someone to take her away. That I'd let that happen. That I wanted Esme to end up with the guy from the park. I tried to speak to him, but Derek stepped between us, his arms across his chest, and shook his head. Blocked. I glared at his betrayal. I'd thought we were friends. He'd shut me out.

I walked out of Rhys's office, my legs unsteady. The hallway grew longer with each step. I slid my hands along the wall to keep myself upright. I gasped in hungry breaths like I'd just clawed my way to the surface of a surging ocean.

I sat on the edge of my bed and I didn't know what to do. *Where would I go now?* I had a lot of money in my account. I could start over. Build a new life for myself, but my stomach soured as I thought about leaving Rhys and Esme. I loved them. I knew that now. I loved them more than I'd ever loved anyone and I didn't want to leave, but there was no way to stay if he thought I'd done something so terrible.

The fact that he thought I'd been working with Killian to

expose his secret made me want to rage back at him. Shatter a few glasses of my own. My anger poured off me in waves. *After everything we'd had together, after how much I cared for Esme, how could he think I could do something so traitorous, so vile?*

Then my rage turned to Killian who deserved it most. Killian, that fucking bastard wasn't going to get away with it. I wasn't above showing him just what happened when someone fucked with my family.

"Ma'am, you can't go in there." A stocky woman in her fifties chased after me. I blew right past her, pushed the solid wood door open, and closed it right in her face, locking it behind me. She pounded on the door, but I didn't give a shit. The time for being nice was over. The breakdown I'd had when I left Rhys's apartment was far from pretty. Everything was ruined. I told him I loved him and he kicked me out. He didn't believe me. But something bigger than us was at stake. The life of a little girl hung in the balance.

"Mel! I certainly didn't think I'd be seeing you so soon," Killian said, his hand behind his head as he leaned back in his chair, like he didn't have a care in the world.

"What did you do?" I asked, through clenched teeth. My hands fisted at my sides. The appeal of punching him in his smug mouth wasn't lost on me. No wonder Rhys went for it that night on the balcony.

"I did what I needed to do to get back what was mine," he said, leaning forward.

"What was yours?" I said, my voice hitching. "You dragged me into this. Made him think I had something to do with you. That I was working for you."

"He should know what it feels like to have the people closest to him betray him."

"I didn't. I'd never do that to him."

"It doesn't matter if you did, it's what he thinks," he sneered. "And when he watches his fortune drain away, everyone will see him for who he really is. Maybe Rachel will see who he really is."

"You dragged her into this, too. You're talking about the money? Who gives a shit about the money?" I couldn't believe that, with lives on the line, he'd care about something so petty.

"It's not just about the money, it's about justice. I'm not going to let Rhys get away with his good guy routine he's been pulling his whole life."

"Money and justice, huh? Justice for who? For you?"

"Yes, for me and for his wife. And everyone else he's fucked over in his life. Everyone who's ever been mixed up with him ends up regretting it. He's thrown around his money for so long, he doesn't know what it's like to deal with the consequences."

"You don't know what the hell you're talking about." I couldn't believe someone so powerful could be so petty.

"He killed her!" he roared, toe-to-toe with me now. "I knew Beth, a scholarship kid like me. And just like he railroaded me and everyone else at our school, he railroaded her. And when she wouldn't agree to whatever plans he had, he killed her." My mind swam as I tried to piece together what the hell he talked about. This story did not fit in with everything happening right now.

"What are you talking about? Were you in contact with Beth?"

"Yeah, she got in touch with me not long before she died.

Said she was wrong about Rhys and needed money to run away. She was going to leave him."

"For you?"

"No, not for me. For Allan. But she couldn't contact him, so she got in touch with me. The three of us were from the same neighborhood growing up. She was like a sister to me."

"Then you knew about her problems? About the drugs?" *How could he think Rhys killed her? He had his issues, but he wasn't a killer.* Killian hand waved it away.

"She was screwed up in all that when we were in school, but she got clean. Cleaned up her life until she married. She wasn't going to toe the line anymore. Be the good little wife he wanted, and he killed her," he said, his eyes fierce and his fists clenched. The tears in his eyes told me this wasn't just some vendetta about money.

"She died in a rest stop bathroom of an overdose, Killian."

"She didn't," he said, looking away from me, shaking his head. "She was clean. Had been for a while, she told me. But he was practically keeping her prisoner. She said he was having her followed."

"He was having her followed because she couldn't keep the addiction at bay. She did have a problem. She was using. She was there in that rest stop with Esme. She brought her little girl there to get high and she died." His head snapped back, the color draining from his face.

"What?" He stared at me like a part of his world had just imploded.

"I'm sorry. I can tell she meant something to you, but I saw the sealed police report, unredacted. She died of an overdose, Esme was with her. Stuck in that rest stop bathroom for hours before Derek found her." He staggered back and I almost felt bad for him. *Almost.* If I hadn't remembered what he'd brought into our lives, upending the quiet tranquility of the life Rhys had built for his daughter.

"That doesn't make any sense. Why would he cover it up? Why wouldn't he let them publish that report?"

"Esme. She'd already been through enough trauma. He didn't want her to have to face that in the news every day of her life. To have other people bring it up and shove it in her face. He did it to protect her. All he's ever done is to protect her and now you've opened a Pandora's box that's going to destroy that little girl."

A thumping and pounding came to the office door. I glanced over my shoulder. I didn't have much time left. Security flung the door open and burst into the office. Three burly security guards grabbed me by the arms and tried to haul me out. Killian held up his hand.

"Stop! Let her go. I'm fine," he said to the guards, who immediately let me go. They glanced back and forth between us. "I said go," he said through gritted teeth, and the guards backed up like they were trying to escape a rattlesnake. He did seem like the type to strike out at anyone who got in his way. And then his focus was back on me.

"You're going to ruin more than Rhys's life with this vendetta built on lies."

"I haven't done anything, except try to expose the crime he committed."

"To protect Esme!" I said, trying to control my anger. "He didn't want it splashed all over the papers about his wife losing her battle with her addiction. He didn't commit a crime. He tried to protect his daughter from the truth of her mother's death. To not have it splashed all over the tabloids for her to read and know about for the rest of her life."

"I grew up in a shitty situation, too. I'm sure being a

scholarship kid at a school where Rhys went sucked, but you know what? I would never hurt a little kid because of some grudge I held against someone."

"He had a hand in her death," he said, anger still pouring off him but his voice softer, almost broken.

"He didn't, Killian. He didn't. She overdosed. She was sick and couldn't get a handle on it. She died and he had done everything he could to protect her from herself. But bringing Allan to challenge for custody? Do you know what that would do to her? How it would destroy her to be taken away from Rhys? Even for a day," I said, slamming my hands against his chest. But he just stood there, completely still, my hands didn't move him an inch.

"What did you just say?" he asked, slowly. And then the room shifted as I realized he didn't know anything about that part.

"Esme isn't Rhys's?" he said, slowly, the words falling from his mouth. *Oh, fuck.*

"You're saying, you didn't call Allan to file for a paternity suit? Didn't try to get him to go after Esme?"

"He did what?" he roared. And he looked every part his nickname. *Kill.*

"He served Rhys a letter demanding a paternity test. You didn't do that?" I didn't know if I believed him. He did have his sights set on completely destroying the man I loved. I didn't think somehow his conscience got to him, but the way the veins in his neck were throbbing, I wasn't sure what the hell happened.

"No, I didn't." He ran his hands through his hair, his muscles bunching under his shirt, like he might burst at any moment. "Fuck," he roared, so loud it made me jump and I'd spent a fair amount of time around temperamental men.

"What did you think was going to happen, Killian? You

didn't think that, if you got your way and exacted your little revenge, it would hurt his daughter? You didn't think about it because all you cared about was the vendetta, not who was swept up in the wake of your destruction. So now, you've put his daughter in jeopardy and, if you think he's going to take that lying down, you'd better think again," I said, my voice hard as steel. Rhys might not want me anymore, but I sure as hell would be whatever I could to protect Esme.

"I'll take care of it," he said, squeezing the back of his neck.

"How are you going to take care of it?"

"I said, I'll take care of it," he growled. "Why do you care anyway? I'm sure, from the way you stormed in here, that he must have fired you. Told you to get out. Why try to protect him?"

"Because he's a package deal. And I don't know what kind of crazy shit I'd do if someone threatened to take my child from me. He might have kicked me out, but that doesn't mean I won't do whatever I can to protect Esme."

"You care that much about a kid who isn't even yours?"

"Yes. She might not be my blood but I'll do whatever I can to protect her. You better fix it because if you don't I'll find a way to hurt you. I might not have your money or your influence, but I swear, I will do everything in my power to end you," I said, completely aware of how much I meant it. I didn't care what I had to do, but if he didn't fix this, I would make him pay.

As for Rhys, I didn't know what to do. He wasn't going to let me waltz into the apartment and tell him what I had found out. I didn't know what I could do to help. Just a few months ago the apartment was a place I'd been afraid to set foot in, unsure of how it would all work. And here I was, exactly where I feared I'd be. I knew it would end. I knew it wouldn't last, but I'd let myself live in that fairytale land where someone like Rhys and I could be happy together. Me, Rhys and Esme, together. A family. And just like before, it had all been taken away from me.

31

RHYS

The next few days were torture. Reporters swarmed the building. There was news on the horizon, a leak about a big story, but no one had the specifics. I watched Esme play in her room, wearing little elf ears pretending her chairs were reindeer. It was only a few days before Christmas. She kept asking where Mel was. When they were going to bake cookies. I didn't know how to tell her. I couldn't form the words in my head, let alone say them aloud. But she was gone and I couldn't let her back into our lives, no matter how much it hurt. The raw angry hurt so much, that I didn't know if I'd ever recover from it.

From the moment they had laid baby Esme in my arms, I knew. Not my blood, but she was mine all the same. I made that choice. I saw the pictures of Beth together with Allan, I knew we hadn't slept together for months before she got pregnant, but I was so ready to have a family. A real family. I wanted so fiercely to make it work that I turned a blind eye when I shouldn't have, and that was the burden I had to bear. It wasn't until the blood test, that the bomb I'd been able to avoid for most of her life, blew up in my face. Then my plans for life after my inheritance changed.

I'd tell her someday soon, but it would be on my terms, not Killian's or Allan's, but mine. I knew what was best for her, she was my daughter. I'd thought about running. Running away with her. But we wouldn't get far, not with my face, not with my reputation and I didn't want to have to take her from everything she knew.

My lawyers were working on getting everything together. Stalling the paternity test. We'd require a court order to make that happen. I'd keep her safe, no matter what. Mel should be here at my side, helping me figure this out. She'd showed me what it was like to have someone there, what Esme was like with a mom in her life. *How could she have done this to us?*

MEL

For the first time in my life I had some money in my pocket. I wasn't worried about where I'd get my next meal, where I would sleep or what my next job would be. I could stand on my own two feet. The dull ache living in my chest, pressing against my heart turned into a sharp stabbing pain when Rhys and Esme crossed my mind. As long as I didn't let them in for too long, it only took my breath away for a few seconds. Not every minute of every day like it had in the beginning.

Christmas had come and gone. I'd been so looking forward to my first one with those two. My presents for Esme had been forwarded to my new apartment. The tears that constantly prickled the backs of my eyes finally spilled over then. He wouldn't even let her have my presents? *Did she think I'd abandoned her? That I'd left without a word?* I never thought I could hate him, but I did as I clutched the pretty pink wrapping paper in my hands. I blocked his number and filtered his email, even though he never called or sent any. I didn't want to be on the receiving end of any angry messages from him.

It had been the first Christmas in a long time that I was actually looking forward to, but I'd made due with what remained. I had enough money in my bank account to start over. Living in the penthouse meant I didn't have many expenses, other than some new clothes. I'd saved almost all I'd made in the time I was there, except for the chunk I gave her to disappear from my life forever.

I wrote letters to Esme every day. I kept them once the first few were returned unopened. I hoped one day I'd be able to give them to her. I tried to call, but every single call went unanswered. I even showed up at the building a few times before security had been informed I wasn't allowed within fifty feet of the entrance.

I held myself back from going to her school. I didn't want to cause a scene. I didn't want to traumatize her. The temptation was heavy. I had to occupy myself when I knew school was letting out, so I didn't find myself waiting across the street for her.

I wrote Killian a check for the money he deposited into my account. I slammed it down on his secretary's desk before rushing out of there. I did not want to have another run-in with him. I still couldn't believe someone could be so callous and vindictive.

Derek dropped my stuff off at my new apartment I shared with four girls I met on an online message board for the college. The rent was manageable and the girls were nice. They were in graduate school or working. Their laughter and nights out made me envy the carefree way they moved through life. Not a care in the world. I stayed in my room and studied for my GED. It took me less than a month to pass it. I'd been so happy, I wanted someone to share it with, but there was no one. I had no one again. It seemed I was destined to only be part of a family for a short time. A glimpse, before I was shuffled back out into the cold.

I signed up for online college classes while I figured out what I wanted to do. I painted a smile on every day, and prayed that one day it would be real. I had everything I'd ever wanted, including my independence, so why did I stay awake at night, staring at the ceiling wondering how it all went wrong? Was Esme getting enough stories before bed? Was Rhys able to sleep or was he back to doing laps in the pool night after night.

I'd been so afraid and ashamed to tell Rhys the truth about me, about my life that I'd lost them both. But he was so quick to believe the worst of me. That's what hurt the most. After everything we'd been through, he didn't trust me. I hadn't seen him since that day. The day everything went to shit. I'd texted every day after I left for the first month. My fingers itched to text after that. I told him everything. How he ripped my guts out that day. A searing, all encompassing pain that radiated through my whole body when he stared at me. Like I was capable of something so horrible.

He hadn't trusted me that night on the balcony, he didn't trust me in the park and he didn't trust me when the money showed up in my account. *How many more times would it take before it was the final straw?* I couldn't take that chance again. I couldn't be with him knowing that at any moment the other shoe might drop. That I might end up even worse off than I was now. What's worse was he wouldn't let me say goodbye to Esme. I didn't know if I could ever forgive that. At least now I had my dignity, well some of it, but would I have it in six months or a year? I'd come begging him on my hands and knees to believe me, every time he thought the worst, if I didn't stop now.

No, I had to stop it now. I deleted the number I'd committed to memory from my phone and I needed to leave it. I'd said everything there was to say. Maybe Esme would find me when she was older. She'd always have a place in my heart.

Days turned to weeks and then it had been a month since I'd left, well, been kicked out. There hadn't been anything in the news about a custody battle. He'd managed to keep things under wraps somehow. He always found a way, didn't he?

Esme's pictures and drawings in the dresser drawer in my room were the hardest to lose. I didn't get to say goodbye. I prayed she didn't think I'd abandoned her. He should have known that would be a knife through my heart. No pictures of her opening her presents at Christmas. Not getting to sit there with a mug of hot chocolate while she opened the gifts I'd picked out for her. I wanted to sit her on my lap, wrapped in our blanket and read those books to her.

January was even worse than usual. The holiday hangover meant everyone trudged through life, waiting for the first signs that winter was ending. The first moment when the sun peeked through the clouded dreariness and the rays of spring felt within reach. Those days weren't there yet. The slush and grime were back after the decorations came down and I went on, trying to make it through one day at a time. I grabbed a cup of coffee from my favorite shop. My weekly treat and sat at the window. People-watching had become my new favorite pastime. I had never seemed to slow down enough to just observe before. I was always running from table to table, interview to interview, disaster to disaster. Here I could sit and pretend I was someone else for a while.

A headline on the paper someone had left behind caught my eye.

Dead. Overdose. The words didn't compute in my mind. It took a long time rolling them over before it made sense. He was dead. Allan was dead. The tightness in my chest relaxed for a second and I could breathe again. I felt horrible that I celebrated the death of a human being, but knowing that Esme wouldn't have to go through some horrendous court battle or run into him again made me think *fuck it*. The fact that he was still using only meant things would have been that much worse for her.

The hustle of the coffee shop did nothing to distract me from the story. He'd died in an apartment owned by Killian Thorne. Killian hadn't been there, but it mentioned they'd grown up near one another. I thought back to our conversation in his office. He said he'd "handle it." Was this his way? After everything he'd done to completely destroy everything Rhys worked for, was he willing to kill to correct his mistake?

I breathed a sigh of relief knowing Esme would be safe with Rhys. No one would be coming to take her away. As much as it hurt knowing he hadn't trusted me, at least she wouldn't have to go through something worse than I had. I ran my knuckles against the ache in my chest. The tightness ebbed a tiny bit.

My phone vibrated on the table beside me. The notification blinked in and out. It was a video message from Rhys, somehow that bypassed the block I'd put on his number. My fingers shook as I picked up the phone. My eyes didn't quite believe what I was seeing. I gathered up my things and raced back to my apartment. Closing my bedroom door behind me, I sat on my bed, knees tucked up to my chest. With fingers of icy dread curled around my stomach I pressed play.

He looked like I felt. Dark bags under his eyes and stubble for days. It looked like he hadn't shaved in awhile.

"I've been trying to give you space, Mel. Trying not to push you to do what I want." His voice rolled over me and I had to close my eyes. I didn't know if I was strong enough for this. "I don't want you to come back to me because you feel you have no other choice. I want you to come back because you can't go on without me. Without us. We miss you."

He rubbed his hand over his face, the sound of his scratchy beard coming through on the video. He missed me now, but what about the next time? What about the next time something bad happened? Would I be kicked out again? Being ripped away from them once hurt so much. I couldn't put myself through that again. My heart pounded in my chest.

"I know this is a chicken shit way of apologizing, but you've blocked my number and haven't responded to any of my emails. I'm sorry, Mel. I'm sorry and I miss you. Esme misses you. This place isn't the same without you. But I understand I screwed up. And I understand if you don't believe in me anymore. I didn't want to apologize like this, but I don't have a choice. Derek's refusing to tell me where you are, even after a threat to force him into daily tea parties with Esme." A small smile curved his lips. Like he was hoping it would make me smile too. "

I love you, Mel. Come back to me." The door to the apartment opened. Laughter and talking filtered in through my closed door. Life went on. Like I wasn't sitting here on my bed trying to hold myself together. Trying to be strong in the face of something I had never before experienced. Someone coming back for me.

Tears spilled down my cheeks and I couldn't wipe them away fast enough. The words I'd longed to hear. The words I thought would save me before and here they were. His face blurred as I clutched the phone against my chest, sobs breaking free as I muffled the sound to keep my roommates from hearing me. They already thought of me as the shut-in, I didn't need them thinking of me as the basket case as well. I checked my email, went to the folder I'd created for any emails from him. I never thought he'd send one, but just in case. There were dozens of emails. One, sometimes two every day. I scrolled through them. He was sorry now, but he had kicked me out. He wouldn't let me contact Esme. What would happen the next time he didn't believe me? I would be in even deeper than I already was. I'd had my heart broken too many times. I couldn't just go back. I couldn't trust that it wouldn't happen again. I couldn't.

32

RHYS

I was barely keeping it together. The last few weeks were like being strapped into a rocket headed straight to hell. My nightmares were back in full force when I managed to close my eyes long enough to sleep.

Every day Esme went to school I feared she wouldn't come back to me. The temptation was so strong to keep her tucked in beside me. Her sadness that Mel was gone was palpable. I didn't know what to do. Everything happened all at once. Killian showing up, Rachel betraying me and then the money in Mel's bank account. I hadn't wanted to believe it, but were my feelings interfering with my ability to see what was really going on? Had I fallen into a trap or had I just made the biggest mistake of my life?

The horizon looked darker than ever. I was hurtling toward the earth from 20,000 feet, bracing for impact and then a parachute appeared out of nowhere to save me. Allan was dead. He'd died of an overdose. With his history, it was an open-and-shut case. The time for the paternity test had been drawn out, using every stalling technique possible to keep it from happening. So as far as anyone knew, he'd been a junkie looking for some quick cash by making baseless accusations against an upstanding member of society.

The minute my lawyers told me he was dead I was in shock. I staggered down the hall to Esme's room and gathered her tiny sleeping frame up in my arms and held her tight. The tears I'd willed back for as long as I can remember came spilling out. I tucked her head under my chin and rocked her back and forth like I'd done all those years ago when she was so tiny in my hands in the hospital. The danger was over, no one would take her from me now.

And as happy as it made me, there was still a part of me that was hollow without Mel. I wanted her there with us to celebrate Christmas and New Year's. I wanted our family dinners to be filled with old diner stories and laughter. And more than anything I wanted to wrap my arms around her and breathe her in at night because I knew, when she was close, the nightmares of my past melted away into the dreams of my future.

I'd let Killian turn me against someone I should have protected. The board elections threw me off and I didn't see how little that mattered. How little the money mattered when my little girl's fate hung in the balance. I expected the next blow to come. The next challenge, but the board election dates came and went without a word from Killian. No bombshell revelation. No eleventh-hour surprises. The boards all voted to reelect me. My birthday came and went. Everything I'd ever wanted was laid out in front of me. The full inheritance, over a billion dollars, at my fingertips, and it all paled when I ran my hand over the empty bed beside me. Cold and smooth instead of a warm, rumpled mess that sometimes elbowed me in the head during the night.

Every time Esme asked for Mel, it was another slice to my heart. I'd driven her away. *How could I make this right?* My last-ditch-effort video message seemed to have fallen on deaf ears. I needed her. We needed her. And I didn't want to do this on my own anymore, and I didn't want to be with anyone else but Mel.

Now that I could breathe again, it was time to finally settle everything with my parents' estate and start the plans I'd had in mind for a long time. The big plans that would finally give me my own freedom, but none of that mattered anymore. My anger at my parents was still there, simmering, but paled in comparison to what I'd lost now. I had left the lawyer's office late that evening, heading to near-midnight dinner with the legal team. Esme hung out with Derek, who turned out to be a much more competent babysitter than I'd imagined. Seeing him decked out with a tiara and his nails painted hot pink was enough to make me think his assignment might need permanent reshuffling. It wasn't like we'd need a security detail for much longer.

I needed a drink, so why not have one on the lawyer's dime? It wasn't like I had anything to go back to in the apartment. Esme would be asleep by the time I got back. I rode over with one of the senior partners. Addison was a cutthroat ballbuster, which was why I'd hired her in the first place. Men often underestimated her because she was beautiful, but I hadn't. I'd seen her chew people up and spit them out on more than one occasion.

As we stepped out of the car, I stepped into a giant icy puddle right outside the door. The frigid water seeped into my shoes. Addison stepped out and I put my hand along her back to guide her away from the water. I'm sure her shoes cost a hell of a lot more than mine. A laughing group of women came toward me, dressed for going out. Addison smiled and thanked me, tugging her coat around her tighter. The group was only a few feet from us now. There were legs for days, but the only legs that mattered were the ones that belonged to Mel, walking toward me. I stopped like the sidewalk had turned to ice and frozen my feet there.

Mel stopped and the group around her paused to see what had grabbed her attention. My eyes were riveted to her. Soaking her in. It had been so long since I'd seen her in person. I had tried to pry her address out of Derek. I knew he'd dropped off her things. But he was enragingly tight-lipped. She looked beautiful. Her hair fell in soft waves around her face, the ends tucked into her coat collar. I wanted to run my fingers through her curls and pull them free from the coat and let them run wild like they always did. Addison and the girls with Mel looked back and forth between us.

"I'll see you inside, Rhys," Addison said, tapping on my arm before heading into the restaurant.

"Mel, you okay?" one of her friends asked, looking from her to me. Mel nodded, she glanced to her friend.

"I...I'm fine. Go ahead and I'll catch up, okay?" Small puffs of her breath formed in front of her face. As the group left, glancing back at us the whole way, I took a couple of steps toward her. I approached her slowly, with caution, as though I was afraid she would scamper off if I moved too quickly.

"Hi," she said, running her fingers over her mouth before glancing up at me.

"Hi," I said, every word I imagined I'd have to say to her in person, gone. I was like a blank slate and everything I'd thought about over the past month died in my throat.

"How are you?" we both said at the same time. My hands

itched to touch her, but I shoved them deep into my pockets. I had my answer when she didn't respond to me. I had my chance. I'd had a taste of the sweetest life I could have imagined and now it was gone. Standing so close to her now almost hurt, a keen piercing stabbed me through the heart that I couldn't touch her.

33

MEL

We stood there in awkward silence. That hurt. Our silences were always filled with so much more. Anger, sexual energy so powerful it nearly knocked me off my feet, happiness, but it had never been awkward before. After living in the apartment for over a month and always turning down their invitations to go out, closing myself off to everyone, I'd finally said yes. My roommates were so excited they all got me ready for the evening. Makeup, hair, the works. I tried not to think of the night of the gala and how one was an exciting next step in a relationship brewing between Rhys and me, and this was an exercise in not becoming a shut-in, trying to forget everything Rhys and I had shared before.

I glanced through the restaurant window at the woman he'd helped out of the car. She was stunning. Her sandy blonde hair done up in a beautiful chignon. Her navy coat showed off her perfect legs and figure. She looked like she walked off the cover of *Powerful Woman* magazine. She sat at a table surrounded by men and she moved with ease. Rhys's equal, someone who knew how to navigate his world. That's exactly what she looked like. I wanted to curl in on myself as I wrapped my arms around my waist. I only had myself to blame.

He'd sent me messages since the video. Tried to contact me and I'd shut him down. I had to imagine women were knocking down his door every day. It wouldn't have taken long for him to find someone else. Someone better. I hoped she was good for Esme. *Did she do the voices Esme liked when she sat on the edge of Esme's bed and read her books? Did he trust her more than he ever trusted me?*

A tear escaped the corner of my eye and I batted it away. *So stupid.* You can't give up on something and then be sad when someone else snatches it up. Embarrassment heated my face.

"Sorry, I'd better let you get back to your date," I said, going around him. His fingers wrapped around my elbow, catching me as I tried to get out of there with a bit of my dignity intact. I glanced over my shoulder, biting my lip to keep it from quivering. That's the last thing I needed, to break down in front of him.

"Mel." He whispered my name as he had so many times before. When he tucked my hair behind my ear, wrapped his arms around me at night or ran his fingers down my spine, his chin nestled against my neck. It raised goosebumps on my skin that had nothing to do with the freezing temperatures. He tugged me closer to him, so close I could feel the heat of his breath on the side of my face. And I looked away, squeezing my eyes shut. "I can barely get myself dressed in the morning now that you're gone. If you think I'd want another woman, you've lost your mind. I only want you, Mel," he said, guiding my face to his. I was caught in his gaze, unable to turn away. The feelings I'd tried so hard to push down, to forget, to leave behind, washed over me and warmed me from the inside out.

The rest was a blur. Our lips intertwined out on the sidewalk, his hands in my hair, tugging on it, just the right edge of painful. I gasped and he delved in deeper, our tongues dancing the way our bodies longed. He flung the door to the SUV open and we fell into it.

"Home," he called out before his lips were back on my skin. Peppering my neck with kisses and nips. I glanced up, relieved Derek wasn't staring back at me. The divider slid up and we were alone.

His hands ran along my legs the entire ride to the apartment. Memories from the gala that I'd tried to forget, but couldn't bear parting with raced through my mind. As excited as I was to see him and as much as I couldn't wait for him to make everything up to me, I wanted to see Esme.

The elevator doors opened and I didn't even waste time taking off my coat. Derek stood from his spot on the couch. Rhys waved him off and I rushed into her room. The dim glow of her nightlight bathed the entire room in pink. There she was. My little girl. I clasped my hand over my mouth to keep my sob from waking her. I gingerly walked into the room and sat on the floor beside her bed. Her little hand poked out of the blanket and off the side of the bed. I wrapped my hands around it and rubbed it between my hands. A drawing tucked under her body. I slid it out and the tears welled back up in my eyes. It was the three of us. Me, Esme and Rhys. Hearts and sunshine filled the paper. I pressed the picture to my chest. She hadn't forgotten.

She opened her eyes and smiled. "Mel, you're back," she said, her eyes droopy.

"I'm back," I said, the tears brimming in my eyes as I smoothed down the hair on her head. "I made pictures for you," she said, her eyes closed and before long she was back to sleep. I didn't even know if she would remember I was there in the morning. I hoped she would because I didn't plan on going anywhere again.

I don't know how long I sat there, but it was long enough that my legs were asleep when Rhys put his hand on my shoulder.

"She drew for you every day," he said, pointing to her dresser drawer that overflowed with drawings. I wanted them.

"And I wrote to her every day," I said, turning back to him. "Can I take them with me to my apartment?"

"Come with me." He held his hand out. I didn't want to leave Esme and I wanted to get her drawings, but I knew we had so much to talk about.

"I've never been anything more than what I can do for people. I've never had someone be there for me, just for me. I...I didn't want to let myself believe in it, Mel. I didn't want to believe because I knew it would kill me if you walked away one day. It would be like I was pushed off a cliff and hitting the rocks, if you ever told me what we had wasn't real," he said, crouched down in front of me, holding my hands.

I knew that feeling. Freefalling was scary when you were used to things working a certain way. When you craved the predictability. I'd never had that luxury. Rhys was a different story.

"I'm glad you told me. I...I know what it's like when you feel like you're freefalling and nothing's going to stop you from crashing back down to earth."

"But I know now and I don't care. I know what it's like living without you and even if it's for one more minute, I want that with you." He kissed our joined hands. His warm lips pressed against the back of my hand. I wanted to run my fingers along his lips. He stood abruptly, leaning against the desk.

"There's more," he said, his hands gripped tightly onto the desk.

"Okay," I said, leaning forward. I needed to know it all and he finally trusted me enough to tell me.

"None of it is mine. The apartment, the cars. It all belongs to the foundations I chair. Given as a perk of the position," he said, shrugging his shoulders. "Everything else, except for a small amount to live off is going to be given to the places I think it will make the most difference. My parents' rules no longer apply. My parents thought I didn't have a charitable bone in my body and that they needed to beat it into me. I just didn't believe in their form of charity. I've got Esme, I've got you, and I've got enough for us to be comfortable without a target on my back, but I wanted to let you know what you were getting into with me," he said, looking unsure. Like I gave a shit about the money. Sure, it was nice, but no one needed as much money as he had.

"I don't care about the money, Rhys. I've got you and I've got Esme and that's all that matters to me," I said, tears filling my eyes. I hated being so freaking weepy. "I'm taking college classes now. Finally, getting around to it after getting my GED," I said, dropping my head. I hated how it made me feel to say it. I should be proud of it. I shouldn't get that twisty gut feeling fessing up to the fact that I hadn't graduated from high school. His fingers caressed my chin. I missed his touch and smell. I breathed him in, and relaxed into him. He tilted my head up until I met his eyes.

"I'm so proud of you. I don't care if you go to college or not, but if it makes you happy. If it's what you want, we're behind you one hundred percent, and Esme and I look forward to embarrassing the hell out of you when you walk across that graduation stage," he said, wrapping his arms around me.

"I'm glad we got to talk. I'm glad you explained it to me. I don't want to forget Esme's pictures. I want to hang them up when I get home."

"Mel, maybe I haven't been clear, but you're home now. This is your home. With us," he said before pressing his lips to mine. His soft lips hard against mine, coaxing the swirling pool of desire back to the surface. I wrapped my arms around his neck, threading my fingers through his hair, letting the silky smoothness run over them.

"Take me to bed," I whispered against his lips. He growled and I chuckled against his lips until he dipped and cradled me in his arms.

"Put me down, you're going to drop me," I said, laughing and pushing on his chest.

"Never again," he said, gazing into my eyes. Tears gathered in his eyes and he blinked them back. "Never," he said, so fiercely that my heart stuttered and the tears were back. All I could do was nod. I believed him.

He laid me in bed like he was afraid I'd disappear. "I love you, Mel," he said as he slid inside me. I gasped, forgetting how good it felt, how good he felt, as I dug my fingers into his muscled back.

"I love you, too," I said on a moan as he slammed into me, thrusting, as I hitched my legs up on his back, our bodies coming together in exquisite bliss I'd never experienced with anyone before and would have with him every day.

This was forever. We were forever.

EPILOGUE

I fidgeted with my dress for the hundredth time since we landed. The car ride over seemed to take just as long as the plane ride. It felt weird to be back on this street again. Rhys convinced me to come. He had looked up their information, although their address was one I'd never forget.

Opening the door to the car, I smelled the flowers from the nearby flowerbed in the air. The garden was bigger than I remembered, sitting out there in the early spring mornings planting bulbs and seeds with Shannon. *What if they didn't want to see me? What if they'd forgotten about me?*

My hands trembled as I pressed the doorbell. I glanced back at Rhys and Esme and gave them something as close to a smile as I could muster. The urge to bite my fingernails made me clasp my hands in front of me. My nails were practically nonexistent after how much I'd gnawed them on the way over. The door swung open and I spun back around, coming face to face with Shannon. Her eyes were wide and she clasped both her hands over her mouth.

"Ben!" she called out. "Melanie," she whispered. I

nodded, my throat too tight to speak. Tears prickled the back of my eyes and tears spilled out onto my cheeks. Shannon stepped out and wrapped her arms around me so tightly I could barely breathe. I brought my arms up and around hers. She smelled exactly the same. The smell brought back every happy memory from my time in this home, and I broke down. Walking back into this house was like I'd returned from an odyssey around the world filled with desperation, heartache, and finally settled into a love that filled me fuller than I had ever imagined possible. But that didn't mean there wasn't still that pain of not seeing them. I couldn't hold back my ragged sobs as I buried my head in her neck. Her arms shook around me as she cried too, her tears wetting my cheek.

"Shannon?" Ben called out from behind her. I glanced up and saw him wiping his hands on a towel. "Mel," he said, rushing toward us before wrapping his arms around both of us and lifting us off the ground. The years had been kind to both of them. I swore they didn't look a day older than when I'd seen them last. Mom and I both laughed, wiping our cheeks as he put us back down. Mom, it felt so right.

"Come in, come in," she said, playfully pushing Ben back inside and waving us in. I glanced back at Rhys and Esme. I was smiling so widely my cheeks hurt. Rhys reached out and slid his hand into mine as we walked into the house. He caressed my wrist with his finger, calming me. I didn't want this moment to end, it was the perfect moment. I was home, with all my favorite people in one place. Everything in the house was the same. The furniture, the paint, the pillows on the couch. They were all as I remembered. When I tried to transport myself back here those times growing up with Colleen, I'd clamp my hands over my ears, rocking back and forth, as drunken high idiots stumbled around my house, or someone locked me out of the house. Sitting on the curb until the street lights came on, waiting for someone to let me in. Sometimes I thought I'd dreamt the whole thing, but now running my hands along the table by the front door, sliding my fingers across the warm wood, it was all real. Everything I'd experienced here. The love, the comfort and the safety. And now I'd made that for myself with the man I loved. I squeezed Rhys's hand and he squeezed mine back.

We passed through the hall, following Mom when Esme tugged on my hand.

"That looks like you," she said, pointing at the pictures on the wall. Framed pictures of my time with them covered the light blue wall. It was still the exact shade of blue I always remembered. Christmas morning, Sunday pancakes, baking, me on the swings, us shooing Ben out of the room when we had our karaoke Fridays. It was all here, up on display. Interspersed among the pictures of me were photos of other kids. There had to be at least ten other kids here. It made me tear up again to know that they hadn't forgotten about me and they'd been able to open their home up to so many other children over the years. Kids who got to experience everything I had with them. I hoped they'd been able to touch each of them as they had me. They'd cared about me just as much as I had for them and they were even more amazing than I'd known before. Mom came up behind me and put her hands on my shoulders.

"Mel, you were always in our hearts. Always. Not being able to see you was the hardest thing we've ever gone through in our lives. We were about thirty seconds from going to jail after trying to track you down and get you back. We hoped that one day when you were ready you'd come to us. That you'd come back home," she said, her voice cracking. I squeezed her hands on my shoulders and glanced back at her, tears gathering in her eyes again.

"I'm glad I came back," I hesitated. She'd always been my mom in my mind, but to say it out loud. "Mom," I said, turning to her. Her tears spilled over then and her sobs rang out in the hall as she wrapped her arms around me and swayed us back and forth. Her tears gathered on my neck, and mine did the same on hers. Pulling back, she ran her hand along my face, pushing my hair back. The smile on her face could have lit a stadium for months and I knew that because I wore the same one.

"You don't know how happy it makes me to hear you call me that, Mel. The daughter of my heart," she said, gathering me up in her arms again. I glanced over at Esme and Rhys. Esme's face was a mask of concern.

"Don't worry, kiddo. These are happy tears," I said, laughing. Rhys produced a stack of tissues for the two of us. Mom told me all about the other kids who'd joined their family over the years. Some lived with them for years, while others were only there for a few weeks or months. Each one had a place on their wall.

"So, who are you, young man?" Ben asked, getting all paternal on Rhys. But Rhys was a good sport.

"I'm Rhys Thayer, sir," he said, holding out his hand.

"Oh wow, I've heard of you. But don't think that lets you off the hook for the grilling that's coming your way about our Mel," he said, shaking Rhys's hand.

"Ben," I said, embarrassed, like any girl would be bringing a guy home to her dad. The pangs in my chest were hitting harder and harder now. These were my parents. They'd done more for me in the short time I'd been with them than they could ever know.

We spent the rest of the day eating, laughing and

hanging out at the house. It wasn't until later that night in the hotel that I finally took a breath. Esme was asleep in her own room in the suite and Rhys sat up against the headboard holding me in his arms, as I reminisced about the entire day and how far we'd come from our first meeting.

"If you'd told me a year ago, I'd be here with you after introducing you to my parents, I'd have laughed myself into a coma," I said, rubbing my hands over his forearms. Their warm, heavy weight helped keep me focused on this moment, on how lucky I was.

"Then I'm definitely glad I didn't tell you a year ago. I'm not into the whole sleeping beauty, unconscious woman thing," he said, into my ear, giving me a nip on the ear. "And since we're already in family expansion mode, what do you think about getting started on a new addition?" he asked, squeezing me tighter.

I glanced over my shoulder at him.

"Are you sure? We haven't even been married a year." I didn't want to rush things. We had all the time in the world and I didn't know the first thing about babies. Esme, I could handle, she could be reasoned with. How in the world was I supposed to be a good parent to a baby?

"You'll be a wonderful mother. You already are to Esme. And the fact that I don't have you pregnant already is only by sheer force of will, and the fact that I knew you needed time. So, what do you say? Do you want to make a baby with me?" he asked, his eyes filled with so much joy and love it took my breath away. How could I say anything but YES! to a man who looked at me like that?

I nodded and that was all it took before he growled and flipped me over, so I sat in his lap.

"How do you want it, Mel?" he said, his cock pressing heavy against my panties.

"Any way you want me. I know how much you love to be in control," I said, licking his lips and grinding myself on his lap. I moaned and he grabbed my ass, squeezing my cheeks as he pressed me down harder on him. His fingers danced across my clit, rubbing it through my underwear. I slid my hands around his neck and up into his hair, devouring his mouth and breathing him in all at once. He lifted me up, slid the crotch of my panties aside and slammed me down on his cock so hard, it took my breath away and I came, my legs shaking, biting into his shoulder to muffle my screams.

He only slowed for a second to let me catch my breath before he lifted me and thrust into me at the same time, driving my pleasure higher and higher. I could tell it would be a long night and I wasn't going to complain one bit. I'd hold on and relish this wild ride. One that only he could create. He'd give me more than I could have imagined. A home. A life where I mattered. A family. It was everything I'd ever been afraid to hope for and it was all laid out in front of me now.

God, I loved this man.

Thank you so much for reading Mr. Control! I hope you loved Rhys and Mel as much as I did! If that's not enough of Rhys and Mel, you can get another speak peek of them in the extended epilogue. Click HERE to get one more day with them!

Do you love enemies to lovers? Enjoy a book that brings all the FEELS and is totally swoon worthy?!

SHAMELESS KING is college enemies to lovers romance that reviewers are saying is full of "raw passion and true banter!"

Grab your FREE copy of the prequel KINGS OF RITTENHOUSE today!

Turn the page for an excerpt of SHAMELESS KINGAnd see their undeniable chemistry unfold in SHAMELESS KING!

If you loved Mr. Control, you'll love the sensual, secret revenge romance, MR. RUIN!

Are you ready for Killian Thorne?! Killian and Rachel's story is the revenge romance you've been waiting for.

"Absolutely brilliant!"

"Can we talk about how hot Killian Thorne is! Wow!!"

ONE-CLICK MR. RUIN TODAY!

And you can sign up for my newsletter to find out all about my newest books and to get the first installment in my newsletter exclusive novella, THE PERFECT VIEW...

Take me to Maya's Newsletter!

Turn the page for an excerpt of SHAMEKLESS KING...

EXCERPT FROM SHAMELESS KING

Makenna

My feet ached as I climbed out of bed, turning off my alarm. I slid on my sneakers, put my hair up into a ponytail. My hair was that weird in between where it wasn't quite red or blonde given the lighting. Checking out the window, I grabbed my phone and earbuds and headed out as the sun rose over the horizon. A run was the perfect way to start the day and get my head on straight.

Transferring as a senior had been a monumentally stupid move. I knew it when I did it, but there were some times when a stupid move made sense. At least in my head. What it didn't do was make graduating on time as easy as it should be. While I had more than enough credits from Stanford, there were certain required courses I needed to take at UPhil, even if I was way past them.

Plus, the BA/MD program meant I was taking some medical school classes since I'd been provisionally accepted. I'd gotten into a similar program back at Stanford. It meant it was only supposed to take me six years to graduate med school by combining some of the course work.

I'd managed to take care of a bunch over the summer, but there was one I had to take on campus. A special course offered only there. *Sophomore Seminar.* Talk about embarrassing. Being in a class full of sophomores as a senior wasn't exactly my idea of fun, but I'd made my bed; I had to lie in it. I'd done everything in my power, bringing in every syllabus from my old courses to show that they were similar and I'd covered similar topics. The deans wouldn't budge.

The circuit around campus took me past a few bleary-eyed people stumbling down the paths that crisscrossed the quad. The warm summer air breezed past me. I wove my way through campus and looked forward to the changing seasons. The vibrant colors of the fall leaves were something I'd missed in California.

Freshly cut grass squished under my sneakers as I took a shortcut back to the apartment. Birds chirped in the morning sky, and it was moments like this that were so perfect it made it hard to breathe.

Moments where I looked around at the flowers and squirrels running up trees and it was like the world stopped moving for a few seconds. The tears always came in those moments. I wiped them away with the back of my hand and picked up the pace past a few guys in rumpled clothes and girls carrying their shoes. Even on a school night, most of the campus had only come back the night before, so there were plenty of walk-of-shamers.

I got back to the apartment, and my roommates were still asleep. Tiptoeing into the kitchen, I made my egg-white omelet and fruit smoothie. There were a few emails from professors with some beginning of the semester notes. I scrolled through my phone, triple checked my schedule, and finished my food. Washing and drying my dishes, I tucked them back into the cabinets and went to my room.

This apartment had been a find. Each room had its own bathroom, which was pretty much unheard of for anywhere a college student would stay. It had been three single efficiency apartments that they combined into one giant one. Tracy and Fiona had needed a third, and I didn't seem like too much of a psycho, in their words, so I'd gotten the spot.

We were still in the I'm-trying-to-figure-out-if-you're-going-to-go-apeshit-and-smother-me-with-a-pillow-in-my-sleep mode, but so far so good. I took a shower, put on the clothes I'd laid out the night before and put on a little bit of makeup. My phone buzzed, and I checked the time. *Perfect.*

I triple checked my books, folders, and binders for each class and slid my backpack on. Glancing at myself in the mirror, I ran my hands over my skirt and pulled my ponytail from under my backpack strap. It was going to be a good day. Making this move had been the right choice. Fine, my parents were traveling across country in an RV and not close by if something happened to Dad, but that was fine. Everything would be fine. I was fine.

My morning classes all went as planned. Senior seminars and labs I needed to meet my graduation requirements were spread throughout the day. The professors had been interested in the work I'd done at Stanford, and there wasn't anything on the syllabi that freaked me out.

After grabbing some lunch in one of the dining halls, where I went over my calendar and put in timelines for completing my projects and lab work, I met up with Tracy, who was still wearing her sunglasses.

"He got everyone to give me a standing ovation when I rolled into class." She sipped out of her thermos, which I was only half sure wasn't filled with booze. "He said if I could make it to class looking like I did, there was no excuse for any of them. I mean, it's not *that* obvious I was super drunk this morning, is it?" She peered at me over her sunglasses.

"Your dress is inside out." I took a sip of my water, trying my best to hold back my laugh.

She glanced down and threw her hands up in defeat. "Damn it. Not again."

Tracy tagged along as I ran a few errands on campus. Somehow her class schedule didn't seem nearly as packed as mine. Stopping by the library before class, I requested a few books I couldn't find online that would help with some of my research during the semester. I also found out when I'd be able to grab a study room. The only wild card in my schedule was Sophomore Seminar.

I figured it would be no problem, but Tracy decided to fill me in. We strolled past people spread out on the lawn on towels even though the sun was setting. A few guys threw Frisbees back and forth without their shirts on, soaking up the last bits of summer we had left.

"Alcott is a notorious hard-ass. He's so pissed off all the time. He was a history PhD student for like ten years and figured once he graduated, they would let him leave the Sophomore Seminar behind. No such luck, so everyone is stuck with his perpetual anger and grouchiness." Tracy's warning came out in hushed tones. The way she spoke, it was like he was a feared sea creature put on the earth to sink a few sophomore GPAs like a kraken from the deep.

"I'm made for those types of professors. I've never had a professor or a teacher I couldn't work with. It won't be a problem." I hadn't maintained a 3.97 GPA by letting a few testy professors get in my way.

"He doesn't accept late work or excuses for anything," she said with her voice low.

I leaned in conspiratorially. "It's okay because I never turn anything in late." And I hadn't. Freshman year in California all on my own, I'd gotten the flu. I wouldn't have been surprised if I'd started bleeding from my eyes. Everything hurt, I could barely keep my eyes open but I managed to turn in my final papers before I drove home for the semester break.

"I'm trying to warn you. Be careful with this guy."

"Thanks for the warning, and I'll make sure I finish all his stuff extra early."

I walked into the room ten minutes before class began. It was usually a pretty good buffer, but the room was packed. My stomach dropped, and I triple checked the time. No, I was definitely early. It looked like I wasn't the only one who'd gotten the memo on Alcott.

The small room was stuffed with desks and fresh-faced sophomores who looked like they were about to be lowered into a vat of acid. His reputation most definitely preceded him. There were only two empty desks available, smack-dab front and center in the room.

The door swung open behind me. Before I could even turn around, something heavy slammed into my back. Tripping over my own feet, I grabbed on to one of the desks to steady myself as I was nearly bowled over by someone pushing me out of the way like I wasn't even there.

"Take your seats," came the gruff voice from the professor. My heart in my throat, I slid into the first empty desk and tried to settle myself. Almost taking a header in front of a class full of sophomores—or anyone, for that matter—wasn't exactly my idea of a fun way to start the semester.

I ran my sweaty palms over my skirt, smoothing it under the desk. Sufficiently de-sweatified, I took out my notepad as the professor hefted his massive bag up onto his desk and took out thick packets of paper and slammed them down on the desk with an ominous *thud*.

Get yourself together! Things were fine. This was fine.

Until they weren't fine. Alcott finished his paper stacking and stood, staring down the whole class, ready to deliver what I could only imagine would be a soul-crushing speech, when the door swung open.

Like I'd conjured my worst nightmare to go along with the professor who already made me hate this class, the last person I ever wanted to be stuck in a class with swanned into the room smack-dab on the hour.

Declan strode into my final class of the day like he walked into every room, chest first. Even into a Sophomore

Seminar where he should be hiding his face, he strode in like he owned the place. My spine went stock straight, and the hairs on the back of my neck rose as his gaze swept over the class and landed on me.

The one empty seat in the closet-sized classroom was beside me. *Of course it was.* He stopped and pivoted like he was thinking of walking right back out before a look of resignation settled over his face. It was probably the same one on mine.

The desk-chair combo scraped across the floor as Declan dragged it away, trying to get a few millimeters farther away from my seat. *Good luck with that.* The desks barely fit as it was.

"This semester because the administration has decided to yet again saddle me with this class, I'm changing things up." Professor Alcott looked every bit the part of a disaffected academic. He wore a tweed blazer even though it was at least eighty degrees in the pressure cooker of a room. The jacket was frayed and thinning in some parts.

"Since I don't want to read all your papers, I'm pairing you up. You will have a partner for the duration of the class. All your assignments will be completed together."

A creeping sense of dread settled over me. *Please not him. Please not him.* The professor called out the names of different students in the class, walking around the room and giving everyone a sheet of paper with their partner's contact information on it.

"Makenna Halstead." I raised my hand. "And you must be Declan McAvoy." He slid the pieces of paper onto our desks at the same time, and my stomach dropped. "Since you two are seniors and have somehow made it this far without passing this class, I wouldn't want to subject you to anyone else. Meet your new partners."

His dig for thinking I had actually failed a class didn't even land because whooshing blood pounding in my ears drowned out everything else except the words *new partners*.

"This is permanent. I don't want to hear any whining about wanting to switch or wanting to be with your BFF or bestie or whatever the hell you call friends nowadays. These are your partners. Don't come complaining to me about anything, unless they are actively trying to murder you. Past attempts don't count. Get the work done. That's the most important thing. In life, you don't get to do a lot of shit you want to do, but you have to make it work."

My hands tightened around the paper he'd sat in front of me. The gentle crunching as I crumpled the edges was the only sound other than the frightened breaths of everyone around me. I refused to look at Declan and kept my eyes on the professor trying to figure out what fresh hell he was ready to unleash on the class. This wasn't going to work. I could not be partners with Declan.

Glancing down at the wrinkled paper on my desk, I smoothed out the edges.

"What's the matter, Books? Afraid my irresponsibility will rub off on you? Look at you, already creasing your papers. Next you'll be coloring outside the lines and maybe even leaving the house without an emergency supply kit for a small village." He glanced down at my bag and backpack combo, and I reflexively followed his gaze. The pen sticking out of his mouth clicked on his teeth, and my gaze narrowed, zeroing in on him, his mouth, and his disgusting habit. Yes, I carried around a lot of stuff, but it was the first day. Preparation was key.

Gritting my teeth, I sat up straight and waited for the professor to finish his droning speech. He handed out the thick packets sitting on his desk, and the mood in the room edged further into resignation that this level of suckage would only grow throughout the semester.

I could handle the workload. I could handle a hard-ass professor. I could not handle putting my GPA in the hands of someone like Declan. *My future.* I'd go to office hours the first chance I got.

"That's all. I'll see you next week after you've turned in your first assignment."

No one moved until the professor closed his bag and strode out of the door, the happiest he'd been since he walked in.

A hot and heavy presence pressed in close beside me as Declan rested his arms on the edge of my desk.

"When do you want to meet, Books?" he said around the chewed-on pen tucked in the side of his mouth. I took a few calming breaths and packed up my stuff.

"Let's try to do this through e-mail and a shared doc online. Maybe that's the best way to handle this." I put on a smile so weak a stiff breeze would have blown it away.

Declan made a *tsk*ing sound that fanned the embers of the annoyance that had been building since he stepped foot in the classroom.

"Check out the first line of the assignment." He slid it across my desk, and I glanced over at it. In big bold letters it read: **YOU MUST MEET IN PERSON. THE WORLD IS MADE UP OF PEOPLE MEETING FACE-TO-FACE. DEAL WITH IT.**

Thanks, Professor.

Declan

Sophomore Seminar was bad enough but ending up partnered with Makenna was a cosmic kick in the balls with everything else going on. But it was almost worth it to be Mak's partner for the look of annoyance on her face. She didn't want to be paired up with me any more than I wanted to be paired up with her, but I'd take pleasure in her irritation.

I held back my laugh as she crumpled her paper and tried to smooth it out. She was so tightly wound it would be a miracle if she didn't have a heart attack by the time she was thirty. Pointing out that we had to meet in person gave me some sick satisfaction that at least this class would be entertaining, if nothing else.

She packed up her giant bags like she was a Sherpa setting out to conquer the treachery of Mount Everest, and I was tempted to help her with them but I figured I might pull back a nub. Walking behind her as we left class, I followed as she rushed out of the building.

People walking by high-fived me or waved, and I waved back but didn't stop because I didn't want to lose Mak, who was walking like someone had started a brushfire behind her.

I don't even know if she was leading us somewhere in particular or storming off, driven by her blinding rage. She might not even have known I was still there from the deep thought grooves creased in her forehead.

"Are we going somewhere in particular? Or were you trying to walk me somewhere private to murder me and secure yourself a new partner."

She jumped at the sound of my voice, so maybe she hadn't remembered I was there. Blow to the ego.

"I reserved a room in the library for after class. I need to be there before five minutes after six or they will give it away."

"Which library?"

"Samuelson."

"Why the hell did you book a library clear across campus when Harbin Library is right there?"

She made an exasperated sound. "Because I didn't know!" She threw her hands up. "I didn't realize the buildings were so far apart when I planned my schedule out for the day, and by the time I realized it, all the rooms in Harbin were booked."

I checked the time, and we had about two minutes to get there. Not really knowing what the big deal was, I didn't want to start things off on an even worse foot with her. Lumbering under the collective weight of a small mining town, she wasn't going to make it there.

"Here, let me help." I grabbed one of the bags off her shoulder without asking. She grabbed for the strap, but it slipped through her fingers. I slung her bag of bricks onto my back.

"Let's go, Books. We've got two minutes." I picked up the pace, and she scrambled behind me to keep up as we wove through the early evening dinner crowd crossing campus. The shining lights of the library up ahead meant the sweat trickling down my back was worth it. I swear she was training for some kind of Iron Man race with this bag.

We both dropped our bags onto the library floor at exactly six minutes after. I went in search of some water. Maybe I should have Mak weight train me. When I came back, the perky, curly-haired student worker behind the desk shook her head as Mak slid her ID card across the counter.

"I came all the way across campus. I need this study room." She held out her ID card to the person on the other side of the counter like she wasn't going to take no for an answer.

"The policy is five minutes."

I stepped up beside Mak, and the girl's eyes got wide. I glanced down at her name tag. *Amanda*.

"But what's a little rule bending between friends, Amanda. It's actually my fault. I was talking to a few people about the upcoming season, and Mak was waiting for me. I held her up, and that's why we were late." I threw on the smile that got me out of all kinds of shit, and she made that telltale giggle-snort thing that let me know I had her.

"What do you say you bend the rules a little and let her have the room?"

The girl glanced between the two of us and sighed.

"Okay, yeah, it's fine." She peeked up at me as she typed away on the computer and took Mak's ID card again. Mak grabbed her bags off the floor and trudged to the elevators after getting her room assignment.

Jabbing the button for the third floor like it had killed her dog, she stood in front of the doors waiting for it to arrive. She crossed her arms over her chest, her shoulders looking like they were going to buckle under the weight of the bags.

"Do I get a thank you?"

"Thank you," she bit out.

"Don't sound so happy about it." I leaned against the wall beside the slowest elevators known to man. "So, what's the big deal about this study room? Why the rush?"

"It's a room reservation for the entire semester, and this is the closest library to my apartment. While my roommates seem fine now, I wanted a place I could go to study if they were too loud. And usually the graduate students snag these rooms early, so I needed to get one right away."

"Gotcha. You really cover all your bases, huh?"

I meant it as a genuine compliment, but she didn't seem

to take it that way, glaring at me as the elevator arrived and the doors opened. I stepped in behind her, and she moved to the far side of the elevator like she'd climbed on board with a leper.

The elevator shook and groaned as it climbed to the third floor. The musty-paper smell was even stronger up here. Half the lights didn't turn on as we passed by. It was almost completely deserted, but the rooms lining the outside of the floor were already filled with stacks of books, personal items, and everything else a person who lived at the library would need.

Mak stopped in front of a room and used her ID card to open the door and stepped inside. The door beside hers swung open, and a blonde popped her head out. Her eyes got big when she spotted me, and her cheeks turned beet red.

"Hi, I'm Angel. It looks like we're neighbors." She stuck her hand out. I hesitated and extended my arm. The stars were already in Angel's eyes, and I wasn't interested, not even a little bit. Our introductions were interrupted when Mak came back to the door.

"He's not your new neighbor. He's popping in for a quick visit." She glared at me and motioned with her head for me to go inside, spinning around and intercepting poor Angel's hand.

"Oh, right. Nice to meet you." She leaned in past Mak and waved to me. "And you too."

Mak closed the door and leaned against it with her arms crossed over her chest. When she leaned back like that, it had the unfortunate—well, not for me—consequence of pushing her tits up even higher. I found my gaze drifting down to them while trying to avoid the face-melting glare in her eyes.

Pushing off the door, she started digging through her Sherpa bags, unloading more books than one of the shelves in this library. I couldn't help but glance at her legs as she bent over to take things out. Nice legs, better than nice, even. Pretty spectacular. Too bad they were attached to someone so full of herself I was surprised she could barely see out her eyeballs.

I stared up at the ceiling because the thoughts I was having were not the thoughts you had about a woman who was probably going to do everything in her power to screw me over that semester, and not in a good way. The one time she'd been cool was one time I tried to forget. It was a mirage.

Maybe if she laid off the homicidal-thought daggers for a bit, we could make this arrangement more fun for the both of us, but I had no doubt in my mind that she would remove my balls with an ice cream scoop if I so much as hinted that I might be interested in anything more than the work.

"Our first assignment is due in a week. Why don't you tell me which parts of this you think you can handle, and I'll do the rest?" She slid the paper across the desk, and I slid it right back to her, my anger shooting up.

"You really think I'm a moron, huh?"

"Listen, we need to get through this. You're the one who's a senior in Sophomore Seminar. What am I supposed to think?"

"You're right there beside me in class, aren't you?"

"As a transfer. If I didn't have to take this bullshit class, I'd be able to graduate before the summer, so I'm not any happier than you are about this. We have to discuss the five strategies and approaches adopted to promote development and reduce poverty over four decades in the country of our choice, and the impact of those strategies."

"Fine. You take two, I'll take three."

"I'll take four, and you take one."

I clenched my fists against my thighs.

"So, you can complain to Alcott that I'm not pulling my weight?" My voice rose as she kept looking at me like I couldn't be trusted not to walk headfirst into a wall without enough warning. She squeezed the bridge of her nose.

"I'm trying to make this easy for you, Declan. Just like everything else in your life. You should be thanking me. I'm not going to rat you out to Alcott. I'm trying to get through this year and graduate as quickly as I can."

"And you see me as a barrier to that. Sorry we can't all be as perfect as you."

She glanced up at me, and something flashed in her eyes. I didn't know what it was, but it was still boiling from her endless digs. Her shoulders sagged, and she sat in the other chair in the room.

"I don't have anything against you personally."

I scoffed, and she peered up at me.

"Fine. I do. You don't know what it's like for someone like me to have my grades in the hands of someone like you."

My hackles rose as she pushed all my buttons.

"Someone like me? And how do you think I feel having my grades and future as a hockey player at this school in the hands of a perfectionist who would sooner watch someone drown than have it mess up their set schedule for life?"

She jerked back like I'd slapped her.

"It seems like we're both relying on someone we don't trust, so we might as well make the best of it and get this shit done so we can see each other for the least amount of time possible." I peered over at the assignment on the desk.

"I'll take two. You take two, and we'll finish the fifth one together. Maybe once you see that I'm not a walking, talking brain donor, you'll loosen the hell up, and we can have an enjoyable rest of the semester."

"Fine." The word barely made it past her clenched teeth.

We grabbed our computers and worked out which country we wanted to highlight and which issues to write about in our paper. With a basic outline for all the items, she seemed satisfied that I wasn't a babbling moron.

"We can meet to go over this stuff on Saturday and get it ready to submit on Tuesday, the day before class." She put her laptop back in the bag that was no longer bursting at the seams since she'd unloaded most of the stuff onto the small shelf above the desk in the study room.

"What time on Saturday?" I slid my arms into the straps of my backpack.

"Three?" She put her bags on her arms and no longer looked like she was going to keel over.

"Three works."

She opened her mouth and snapped it shut before turning to the door. I followed behind her and almost ran her over when she stopped short and whipped around with her mouth opening and closing again before she stared up at me.

"Spit it out, Books."

She shot me a quick glare, and the corners of her mouth turned down.

"I'm sorry if I made you think I thought you were stupid. I don't. I... This class is really important to me, and I need to do well."

I stared at her.

"I need to do well too. It's the only way I get to play with my team. I'm not going to screw this up."

"Then I think things will go well this semester." She held

out her hand, which was probably the only time since that one night she'd ever willingly touched me. I slid my hand into her soft, warm one with her delicate fingers wrapping around mine.

The charged air between us shifted as we both let our guards down a little. The blue in her eyes behind those glasses seemed even brighter under the fluorescent library lights, and the pink of her lips was still shiny from when she'd been nibbling on them while we worked through our research.

"I think so too." We stood there, shaking our hands until one of the doors on the floor slammed shut. She jumped like she'd come out of a trance and whipped around, rushing from the room, and I once again had to chase after her. I didn't know how long we shook hands, but it was long enough that even as we left the library and parted ways, I could still feel her gentle touch wrapped around my hand.

I squeezed the back of my neck and shook my head as I caught a shuttle back across campus. If there was one person not to get any illusions about being anything more than study partners with, it was Makenna. The Ice Queen would eviscerate anyone who tried to get close.

Makenna

Standing outside the professor's office, I shifted from foot to foot. It had taken me two days to build up the courage to even come near his office. I couldn't get the study session with Declan out of my head, and that was not a good thing.

When we'd shaken on it at the end and his hand enveloped mine. The calluses from his fingers had scraped against my skin and sent a shiver through me.

I'd noticed his freckles before, but up close the smattering of light brown flecks looked like they had been strategically placed for maximum impact. Like the cosmos created just the right combo to make unsuspecting women get lost staring at the pattern. The way they streaked across his skin reminded me of a lake on a warm summer's day.

The handshake had gone on for longer than it should have, and I didn't like how it made me feel. It made me want to laugh, like a giddy girl. Like Angel, who'd annoyingly checked in on my study space every time I was there, craning her neck to see if Declan had also stopped by.

With Saturday creeping closer through the week, my anxiety had spiked. I'd even changed our meeting time twice trying to put it off a little longer. It was the dream I had the night before of our dance back at prom that spurred me into action.

I'd dragged myself down to Alcott's office. That giggly, bubbly feeling was scarier than any of the other shit going on in my head. Declan was everything I'd sworn I'd never be. He took everything for granted and never seemed to take anything seriously except for hockey.

Declan was a heat-seeking flirt missile. If there was a pulse, he'd turn on his charm to get what he wanted. I wasn't going to let him flirt his way into screwing up my graduation and med school plans. They were too important. Not just for me but for Daniel.

The office door swung open, and a girl with her hair in a braid came shuffling out, clutching her backpack straps. She glanced up at me with a scared look and trudged her way down the hall.

My hands were clammy, and my stomach threatened to revolt as I glanced from the door of doom to the girl who looked like someone had kicked her puppy and then kicked her. I took a step back, and my shoes squeaked on the floor. My shoulders hitched up around my ears, and I contemplated climbing into my backpack and pretending I'd never been there.

"I can hear you out there. Come in so we can get this over with." Professor Alcott's snarky voice boomed in the empty hall, and I glanced around, looking for a path of escape. Before I could fling myself out the nearest window, he popped his head out into the hallway and actually rolled his eyes when he saw me.

"I wondered how long it would take you to show up. Come in." He waved me into the office, and I walked like a tin soldier brought to life. My legs were as heavy as lead, and I swore the beads of sweat rolling down my back were forming a nice little swimming pool for me to drown myself in later.

Alcott dropped into his chair and leaned back, lacing his fingers together and sliding them behind his head. Kicking his feet up on the desk, he closed his eyes as I sat in the chair on the other side of his desk. The room smelled like old books and desperation, which was fitting because I'm sure that was the same thing people thought about me.

"If the first words out of your mouth are asking for a partner change, I can fail you both right now."

His words sent a bolt of fear through me, and my bouncing leg stopped immediately.

"Or did you come here for the amazingly charismatic company." He lifted one eyebrow.

"No. Of course not. I mean, I'm not here to change partners. I wasn't talking about the company part." *Is it hot in here?* It felt like the office had been launched into orbit around the sun. I barely stopped myself from tugging at the collar of my shirt.

Alcott dropped his feet down and tented his fingers on the top of his desk.

"Spit it out. Why are you here then?"

I opened my mouth and snapped it shut.

"I wanted to know if the noon deadline for the papers was Eastern Time or in another time zone." I cringed inside but managed to keep a straight face as he looked at me like I'd suddenly turned into an even more moronic little kid.

"It's all spelled out for you in the syllabus, but sure, why the hell not? It's twelve noon on the deadline day. I learned my lesson with midnight deadlines. Apparently, college students have a hard time figuring out which day midnight assignments are due. The portal shuts down at exactly 12:00:01p.m., and no late assignments will be accepted. Does that answer your question?"

I nodded and grabbed my bag. Standing, I slid it onto my back. He smirked at me with that smug look of his, and the pit in the bottom of my stomach grew.

This was it. I was partners with Declan for the rest of the semester. Taking a deep breath, I reached for the doorknob and opened it. Halfway in and halfway out of the office, I skidded to a stop when Alcott called my name.

"Ms. Halstead, if you had a truly compelling reason—and I'm talking incredibly exceptional reason—for changing partners, I might entertain it."

Frozen in the doorway, I thought of why I didn't want to work with Declan. High school drama and hating his attitude didn't feel like they fit the bill of exceptional in this case. Neither did *I get butterflies in my stomach when he touches me.* I turned around to face Alcott.

"Thank you for letting me know. I don't think it will be an issue."

"Good. Now close the door." And just like that I was dismissed.

Making my way across campus, I found myself back at the library like I was a homing pigeon, and this was my starting point. Climbing the steps, I wandered to my study room, opening the door when the one beside me popped open. Angel popped out with a wide smile. It dimmed slightly when she saw I was alone.

"Hi, neighbor," she said so cheerily I expected gumdrops to come pouring out of her mouth.

"Hi, Angel." If I didn't stand out there and talk to her for a few minutes, she would follow me inside. I'd learned that over the past few days.

"What are you up to this weekend?"

"Nothing. Working on my assignments. Going for a run. Sleeping." Taking a deep breath, I asked the question even though I really didn't want to. "What about you?"

"Oh, this weekend will be amazing. I'm going to a concert at the Electric Factory, and then I'm going kayaking with some friends. Then we're thinking we'll probably wander around the city looking for the best cheesesteak, maybe go dancing somewhere.

"I don't have everything planned out yet, but it will be awesome. I need to get all this energy out before the semester really gears up and I'm trapped inside." She said it all in less than two breaths and spent the entire time bouncing on her toes like she had to pee. I didn't really have much to say other than that. Her perpetual peppiness threatened to give me a toothache, but I envied her ease and happiness.

"That sounds really cool. I hope you have a great time." I mustered up my best approximation of a smile.

"You too, with your...run."

Yes, I knew my weekend sounded like the kind of weekend you had when you were being punished, but it would help me get a handle on what had already been a difficult new semester. She disappeared out of my doorway, and I finally felt safe enough to drop my bag and unload my stuff. Leaving Stanford had been a mistake, I'd tried to deny it, but there it was, and now I had to deal with it.

"She's a bubble of energy, isn't she?" A deep voice came from the doorway. My head whipped up, and there was a guy standing at my door, leaning against the door jamb and staring over toward Angel's room.

"That she is."

"I swear, I can hear her pep from across campus." He was in a dark black T-shirt and jeans. Jet-black hair and dark brown eyes. He was like the polar opposite of Angel.

"I'm Seth." He stepped into the room with his hand out.

"Makenna." I shook his soft, strong hand and didn't feel like I was going to keel over any second.

"She's in my master's program. The poor professors don't really know what to do with her. Mechanical engineering programs aren't exactly built on the woohoos and excitement of other programs, but she knows her stuff, so…" He shrugged.

"She seems really nice. I'm not used to that much sunshine."

His rich chuckle filled the room. "Me neither. Listen, I'll leave you to it, but I'm right next door. If you ever need a rescue from happiness overload, let me know."

"I'll bang my head against the wall to alert you before I slip into a sugar coma." I smiled and crossed my arms over my chest, perched on the edge of my desk.

"Or you could give me a call. If you had my number."

Everything in the room stopped like someone hit pause

on the remote. *Is he asking for my number? Is this flirting? How can I not even spot flirting?*

"If you wanted it, that is?" A look of uncertainty passed over his face, and he backed up.

I reached out and shouted louder than I intended. "No!" The red flush crept over my skin like a blanket ready to smother me with my awkwardness. I cleared my throat. "I mean, yes. Sure, I'll take your number, and you can have mine."

"Great." He slid his phone out of his back pocket, and I grabbed mine out of my bag, opening up a new contact. He did the same, and we traded numbers. There was a small flip in my stomach. It wasn't as big as the one I'd gotten with Declan's hand in mine, but I brushed that aside. Seth went back to his study room, and I sat at my desk staring at my books.

After checking through my online calendar, I read over some more assigned pages for the next few weeks but focusing was nearly impossible. My restlessness threatened to boil over as the sun set, filling the study room with oranges and reds. I needed to run.

My assignments for the next week were finished. My part of the research for the Sophomore Seminar paper was long done and proofread twice. Meeting with Declan tomorrow meant my game face had to be on.

I needed to get outside and feel the breeze across my skin. Careful not to alert Angel that I was leaving, I stepped out of my door, only to see the rest of the study rooms completely empty. I checked the time again. After eight.

On the walk back to my apartment, my phone buzzed in my bag. I fished it out, wondering if maybe it was Seth, when relief washed over me.

"Hey, Mom, how's the open road?"

"It's great, sweetheart. I'll send you some pictures. We went to Disneyland yesterday."

I cracked a sad smile as I remembered our one and only visit to Disney World down in Florida.

"Did you get pictures with Mickey?"

"Sure did. Pushed some little kids out of the way to do it, and it was so worth it." Dad's voice came in over the line.

"Hey, Dad."

"Hey, chickadee."

"How are you doing?"

"I'm great. Never better. Your mom and I are going out for dinner and dancing tonight, and then we're off to Vegas tomorrow."

Dinner and dancing. It was like being put back into a time machine. They sounded so happy it almost hurt. I rubbed the achy spot in the center of my chest as I walked along the sidewalk to the cluster of apartments mainly rented by students.

"That sounds awesome. I'm so glad you two are having fun." I'd keep the brightness in my voice if it killed me.

"So are we, and I hope you're not working too much. You're always so hard on yourself. Don't be afraid to have a little fun sometimes."

"I'm not. I have fun."

"Running is not fun," Dad said, sounding highly offended.

"It's fun for me."

"Something not running or school or work related," Mom, unhelpfully, threw in.

I opened my mouth for a comeback, but I didn't really have one. Those things were my life. Pretty much all of it.

"I know we're not there, but we'll be back for Thanksgiving and if you haven't had any fun before then, we're going to burn your textbooks."

"Dad, that's like burning ten thousand dollars. I don't think you want to do that."

"I want you to let yourself live a little. Don't make us park this RV outside your apartment and make sure you have fun."

While the threat was ominous, I kind of liked the idea of them hanging out on campus. I'd be able to see them more, but it would get in the way of *their* newfound lease on life.

"I solemnly swear that this semester I will try to schedule at least a little fun and frivolity."

"You better. We love you!" they both said, laughing the entire time.

I still couldn't wrap my head around their change. Who knew it would take a diagnosis like Dad's to finally snap them out of their haze and rejoin the land of the living. Not that my way of coping was any better. *Perfect match.*

I shoved my key into the lock of my apartment, took a deep breath and closed the door behind me. Bright and playful chatter filled the place. Tracy and Fiona fought over the bathroom mirror at the end of the hall. Dropping my bag in the door, I leaned against the wall and watched them primp and preen, unable to control my smile.

"Makenna, you're back. We were wondering if we'd have to send a search party out to come find you." Tracy turned to me and waved the curling iron in my direction.

"I was hanging out at the library."

"On a Friday? You're not going out?" Fiona said from behind her with an eyeliner pencil precariously close to her eyeball.

"I'm going to go for a run."

They both turned to me with various beauty products clutched in their hands.

"But why?" Tracy wrapped the curling iron around her hair.

"Why are you two crammed into that bathroom when you both have your own?"

"Fiona's has much better lighting than mine." Tracy lined her lips and puckered up in the mirror. Leaving them to their prep, I went into my room and changed into my running gear. Snagging my phone off my bed, I slipped in my earbuds.

"I don't know how long my celibacy challenge is going to last," Fiona said, walking past my door.

"We made the challenge like eight hours ago," Tracy said from the living room. I tried to hold back my laughter and failed as the front door closed behind them. It would be an interesting semester for more reasons than I'd imagined.

After they left, I took off down the street until I made it to campus. Hordes of freshman wandered in search of the mythical college parties, though most people were still getting ready to go out. Always count on the freshman to be early.

My heart pounded as my feet slapped against the concrete, and I let my mind blank. There was nothing but the pavement and my muscles pumping as I wove my way through the streets surrounding campus. The tightness in my chest lessened and the weights of everything going on around me fell away as my legs loosened and hit their stride.

I don't know how long I ran, but I had to duck and dodge through crowds of people heading to the bars or out to beginning-of-the-year parties. Sweat poured off me as I walked back into the apartment. Music filtered in through the walls as other people had their own parties. After taking a shower, I curled up in bed and closed my eyes.

Tomorrow was another day. I'd be face-to-face with Declan again and I needed to make sure I didn't let him get under my skin, but part of me knew he was already there and had been for years.

Ready to see what happens when the Cocky College Hockey Superstar and Fiery Ice Queen can't stop the undeniable chemistry between them? Grab your copy of SHAMELESS KING Today!

AFTERWORD

I wanted to take a moment to acknowledge all of the amazing families out there who can take a special role in a child's life as foster parents. So many times we hear the worst about the system, but there are some truly amazing families who do everything they can to welcome children in need into their homes and hearts.

For more information on how you can change a child's life and become a foster parent, visit the U.S. Department of Health & Human Services to find out about the process in your state.

ACKNOWLEDGMENTS

Sitting down at my keyboard and writing are only a small part of what it takes to create a book. Rhys and Mel have lived in my head for a long time, so I'd like to thank the following people for their help in bringing these characters to life.

My husband for wrangling the kids, so I could grab a little down time here and there to gather my thought and type away.

To my editors, Tamara, Bex and Donna, you are an amazing team and I can't wait to work with you over and over until you're sick and tired of me!

To LJ at Mayhem Cover Creations for my kickass cover, you are so patient, especially when I have you tweaking things down to the wire :)

To my readers, thank you for reading my books. Thank you for the emails and messages telling me how much you love my characters and I'm so looking forward to bringing you even more amazing ones in the days, months and years to come!

Lots of love,
Mx

ALSO BY MAYA HUGHES

Misters

Mr. Ruin - Revenge Romance

Mr. Wicked - Second Chance Romance

Under His Series

Under His Ink - Second Chance Romance

Breaking Free Series

Blinded - Second Chance Secret Baby Romance

Mixed - Enemies to Lovers Romance

Served - Enemies to Lovers Romance

Rocked - Rockstar Romance

Standalone

Passion on the Pitch - Sports Romance

CONNECT WITH MAYA

Sign up for my newsletter to get exclusive bonus content, ARC opportunities, sneak peeks, new release alerts and to find out just what I'm books are coming up next.

Join my reader group for teasers, giveaways and more!

Follow my Amazon author page for new release alerts!

Follow me on Instagram, where I try and fail to take pretty pictures!

Follow me on Twitter, just because :)

I'd love to hear from you! Drop me a line anytime :)
https://www.mayahughes.com/
maya@mayahughes.com